"No!" Hobie cried in alarm, feeling the ground underneath him rumble and shake. *"Not another earthquake!"*

A canoe paddle fell from the rafters above, and he blocked it with his arms. Then an empty gasoline can crashed onto his head, followed by a small cardboard box. So many things were coming at him so fast—it was impossible to move!

Then it happened. The heavy wooden shelves against the wall tipped over—and landed right on top of him!

Hobie felt a flood of pain rush through his legs. He pushed against the shelves, trying to move them. But it was no use. He was trapped!

"Help!" he cried. But there was no one to hear him. No one even knew he was there in the garage...

Dive into the action with the

JUNIOR LIFEGUARD

BAYWATCH series!

- #1: *Hobie Gets a Life*
- #2: *Earthquake!*

And coming in early July 1996:

JUNIOR LIFEGUARD

BAYWATCH series:

- #3: *The Haunted Tower*
- #4: *The Big Wipe-out*

Another Baywatch™ series you'll enjoy from Random House Sprinters™:

BAYWATCH

- #1: *Infatuations*
- #2: *Wet 'n' Wild*

And coming in early July 1996:

BAYWATCH

- #3: *Girls Only*
- #4: *Shark's Cove*

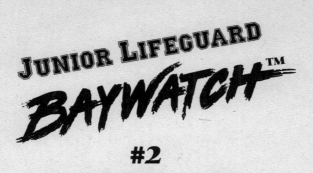

JUNIOR LIFEGUARD
BAYWATCH™

#2
EARTHQUAKE!

by Casey Brady

**Based on a teleplay by
Michael Berk**

**Based on the television series created by
Michael Berk & Douglas Schwartz and
Gregory J. Bonann**

BULLSEYE BOOKS
Random House 🏠 New York

A BULLSEYE BOOK PUBLISHED BY RANDOM HOUSE, INC.

Library of Congress Catalog Card Number: 95–72451
ISBN: 0–679–88116–6
RL: 4.0

Photographs © The Baywatch Production Company.

Printed in the United States of America 10 9 8 7 6 5 4 3 2 1

CHAPTER ONE

Hobie Buchannon squinted against the sun as the other in-line skaters bladed around him. The sky was blue, the temperature was perfect...and on top of that, it was a Saturday.

Hobie grinned. He loved weekends. Actually, he lived for them! Especially three-day weekends, like this one. And he had the perfect day planned: he was going to spend the morning blading and the afternoon rehearsing with his band.

Today, all of the skaters had pledged to skate five miles to raise money for a program called W.A.T.E.R., which would give inner city kids a chance to learn all about the ocean that summer. So far, the Memorial Day weekend event looked as if it was going to be a huge success.

Guys wearing long black shorts skated with girls in colorful bikinis. People were blading forward, backward...some were even doing spins and turns. Hobie watched as one guy jumped up on a ledge, skated down it, and hopped off, jumping into the air before he landed cleanly on the other side of the path.

Hobie didn't skate that well yet, but he planned on becoming an expert someday. It was just that right now, he spent most of his time in the water, swimming and surf-ing.

Hobie's friend Samantha was skating beside him, wearing white shorts and a flowered T-shirt. Ahead of them, Baywatch lifeguard Matt Brody skated with some of the kids he was going to work with in the W.A.T.E.R. program. Hobie and Matt were good friends, even though Matt was a few years older. They hung out a lot together, especially when Hobie was spending time down at Baywatch headquar-ters, where his father, Mitch, worked.

Hobie grinned at his dad as he passed him on the bike path. As usual, Mitch was sur-rounded by women. They were all hanging onto him as he skated along.

Hobie wasn't exactly sure why women went so crazy over a guy like his dad. But Hobie figured there might be hope for him if his dad was such a babe magnet. Maybe it was in his genes. And once he and his band got popular, he'd have girls falling all over him, trying to get his autograph, asking him for dates...

Suddenly, Hobie felt somebody pounding

him on the back with drumsticks, as if he were a snare drum.

"Hey, man, quit it!" Hobie wheeled around and skated backward, trying to grab the drumsticks away from his friend J.B. He couldn't believe J.B. was actually skating with them.

J.B. laughed. "You've got a horrible sense of rhythm anyway, you know?" He nudged his buddy Conner, and the two of them started cracking up.

"Ignore them," Samantha said, skating up beside Hobie and grabbing his arm for support. "You're the best singer we've ever had in our band and they know it."

"Really?" Hobie asked eagerly. "You think so?"

Samantha nodded. "Definitely. And when we cut our first CD, everyone's going to know how great we are."

Hobie could see it now...his face on the CD cover, posters of him plastered all over the stores, his vocals playing nonstop on radio stations...and then there'd be the concerts. He'd walk onto the stage and girls would shriek at the top of their lungs: "Hobie! Hobie!"

Of course, he wouldn't let it go to his head. Not too much, anyway.

He turned around and started focusing on

his skating, darting in and around the other bladers on the path. It didn't matter who crossed the finish line first, since it was a skate–a–thon for charity, but Hobie liked going fast anyway. He felt incredibly cool as he wove his way from left to right, zigzagging to the finish line.

He cruised over the finish line, pumping his fist in the air. "Yes! Come on, guys!" he called back to his friends. "Let's go!"

"Go where?" Conner asked, skating up to him with J.B.

Samantha, following right behind the guys, took a few seconds to catch her breath. She looked at Hobie. "The garage, right?"

Hobie nodded. He and his friends were using his Dad's garage as a practice space for their band. That was totally cool, because it was their own private place—with no parents telling them to turn the volume down!

"Hey, guess what?" Hobie said. "Just now, when I was skating, I got an idea for a new song."

"Let's do it!" J.B. cried, tapping the drum-sticks against his knee.

Just then, Mitch skated up to the group. Two beautiful women in bikinis—different ones this time—were holding onto his arms. "Wh-whoa!" Mitch said, pretending to have trouble stopping so that the women clung even tighter to him. They just laughed.

Mitch smiled when he finally managed to come to a complete stop in front of Hobie. "Julie, Cheryl, have a nice day, thanks a lot," Mitch told the girls. "I couldn't have made it without you!"

The two women in bikinis waved good–bye and skated off, disappearing into the crowd on the pier.

"What's the deal, Dad?" Hobie asked. He looked up at his father, who was wearing shorts and a sleeveless T–shirt. Mitch had the same dark brown, curly hair as Hobie—but his eyes were blue instead of brown, like Hobie's. "You blade better than any of us."

"*I* know that, and *you* know that," Mitch said. "But *they* don't know that." He winked at Hobie.

"I gotta remember that one," J.B. muttered in amazement.

"Me too," Conner agreed, nodding.

Samantha sighed. "Men! So, Hobie—are we going to practice or not?"

"Well—yeah, sure. Sorry, Dad, I gotta go. See you at dinner!" Hobie said, shoving off with his friends.

Mitch stepped in front of Hobie, blocking his path. "Whoa, wait a minute," he said, hold–

ing up his hands. "What about Junior Life-guards? Don't you have to go today?"

Hobie shrugged. "Um…we kind of decided not to do junior guards this summer."

Mitch looked startled by Hobie's announce-ment. "You did?" he said, frowning. "Who decided that?"

"We all decided…as soon as we got a place to rehearse," Samantha said. "You know, for our band?"

J.B. knocked on the trash can beside him with his drumsticks. "Yeah, forget being Junior Lifeguards. We're gonna jam all summer!"

"*You* might be jamming," Mitch said, "but Hobie's not."

Hobie stared at his father. What was he talk-ing about? "Yes, I am."

"No, you're not," Mitch replied.

"Yes, I—" Hobie began to protest.

"Excuse me," Mitch interrupted. "Could I have a little word with my son for a second?" He flashed a smile at Hobie's friends. "Thank you."

Hobie stepped away from the group.

"Dad. I can make my own decisions," Hobie said in a low voice. He hated being told what to do—especially in front of his friends! It was so embarrassing.

"Not decisions this important," Mitch said.

"*What?* You get to make all the important decisions in my life, and I just get to stand there, salute you, and follow orders...is that it?" Hobie asked. Talk about having a strict father. It wasn't fair!

"Hobie, I'm not telling you not to play with your band. I'm just saying..." Mitch ran his fingers through his hair. "Don't give up everything else in your life to do it. Especially junior guards! That's really important."

Hobie kicked the heel of his skate. Junior guards didn't feel so important. Being in the band—singing, writing music, playing keyboards—was much more important to him right now. He'd talked about it with his mother and she understood. So why couldn't his dad?

"Mom said I didn't have to be in junior guards if I didn't want to. She said if I want to be a musician, I should go for it," Hobie said.

Mitch looked shocked. "And when did your mom say that?"

"On the phone, last week," Hobie replied calmly. *So there!* "She said I didn't have to follow in your footsteps. I can do anything I want with my life!" Hobie turned to his buddies. "Come on, we're out of here."

"Hobie!" Mitch called as the group skated away. "Wait, let's talk about this!"

But Hobie didn't turn around. There was no rule that said he had to be a junior guard this summer, or a lifeguard when he got older. Not that it was a bad thing to do or anything.

But Hobie Buchannon was going to be a rock star someday—the sooner, the better.

CHAPTER TWO

"Hey there!" C. J. Parker greeted Mitch as she passed him on the way to her lifeguard tower at the beach later that morning.

"Hey!" Mitch replied, managing a weak smile. It was always good to see C.J., no matter how bad a mood he was in. She managed to cheer him up more often than almost anyone else—probably because they'd been good friends for so long.

"So, did you feel that earthquake this morning?" C.J. asked, stopping beside Mitch, who was pulling off his in-line skates.

C.J. was wearing the standard red one-piece L.A. County lifeguard swimsuit...but on C.J., nothing was standard. With her long blond hair and fantastic figure, she was the very definition of the classic "California girl." And her sense of style almost matched her sense of humor. Mitch was glad to have C.J. working with him.

"Earthquake?" Mitch grumbled. "I didn't feel

9

anything." Right now he was too busy feeling the sting of Hobie rejecting Junior Lifeguards. Didn't his son realize that being a lifeguard was more important than being in a band? Hobie's band wasn't even that good. Not yet, anyway.

"The quake was a four. You didn't feel it at all?" C.J. asked. She flicked her long blond hair over her shoulder.

"C.J., I grew up here," Mitch replied. "I don't feel anything under a six."

"Well, *I* do. My entire bed almost collapsed!" C.J. said. "I mean, who needs an alarm clock with earthquakes happening in the middle of the night? Are you *sure* you didn't feel it?" She sounded almost suspicious.

"C.J., I really didn't," Mitch said with a laugh. "I've got bigger problems on my mind. Like Hobie."

"Oh." C.J. looked sympathetic. "Well, teenagers are probably worse than earthquakes. At least, I know I was." She walked off down the beach toward her tower, and Mitch laughed. He could just imagine C.J. when she was Hobie's age. She must have been a terror!

Mitch headed up to Baywatch headquarters, the command post where everyone checked in before working the beach. As he crossed the deck, one of his coworkers, Lieutenant

Stephanie Holden, came running up from the beach, her hair and off duty blue–and–green bathing suit wet from the ocean.

With her was a man Mitch didn't recognize. Stephanie and the guy were laughing and pushing each other. Even though Stephanie and Mitch hadn't been a couple for a long time now, he still felt jealous when he saw her with someone else. He couldn't help it.

"Mitch!" Stephanie called cheerfully. "Meet Riley Ferguson. Riley, this is Mitch Buchannon."

"Mitch, how are you doing?" Riley asked. He had a bit of a Southern drawl to his voice.

"Good to meet you." Mitch shook Riley's hand. Riley was tall, with short brown hair and a close–cropped beard. He seemed like a nice enough guy, Mitch thought.

"You too," Riley said with a friendly smile.

"Riley's an oceanographer, and he's here with a team of geologists," Stephanie informed Mitch. "They're going to install a seismometer to measure the intensity of the tremors in the Malibu Fault."

"Gotta make sure you guys don't end up becoming ocean lifeguards in Arizona," Riley joked.

"Are you talking about California falling into the ocean?" Mitch asked. He hated people who made jokes like that. It wasn't ever going to happen. At least not while he lived in California. It was something people from out of state always said—almost as if they'd be glad when California did fall into the ocean!

Riley shrugged. "Well, let's just hope it never happens!"

Stephanie smiled at Riley, gazing into his eyes like an adoring puppy. "Riley's specialty is deep-sea diving."

"Really?" Mitch twisted the top off a bottle of mineral water. "Hardhat or scuba?"

"Both. But if I had my choice, I'd free-dive," Riley said.

"*Ooo.*" Stephanie looked at Riley. "I would *love* to learn how to free-dive sometime," she gushed.

Mitch thought he was going to be ill. He'd never seen Stephanie kiss up to a guy like this before. And all over something as basic as being a skin diver?

"It's the closest thing to living under the sea," Riley told her. "Makes you wish you had gills. Ever try it, Mitch?"

"Me?" Mitch grinned. Riley was trying awfully hard to impress Stephanie. "Oh, yeah. Sure. But the thing is, I actually started developing gills…so I had to cut back." He took a long drink of water.

Stephanie frowned at Mitch and rolled her

eyes. "I'm going to the fault with Riley and the two geologists tomorrow. We leave at three in the morning, so we should be back by noon."

Mitch folded his arms across his chest and stared at Stephanie. "Oh, really?"

"Their permit *requires* a safety officer to be there," Stephanie told him.

"And you...volunteered?" Mitch asked. "Just like that?"

"Yes," Stephanie said defiantly. She turned to Riley. "Come on, Riley. Look, I'll need to go over the details of your dive plan with you. Maybe we could do it over dinner at my place."

"Great," Riley drawled. "But I gotta warn you, I'm a vegetarian," he added as they started to walk off.

"Good!" Stephanie grinned. "I make an incredible black bean salad."

"Nice to meet you! Don't work too hard!" Mitch called after them. He had a feeling those two wouldn't get any work done at all. "Black bean salad," he muttered under his breath. *Right!*

Out of the corner of her eye, C.J. spotted a group of swimmers standing at the water's edge: three young women and two men.

When one of the women shouted, "Go!" they all sprinted into the water, laughing and screaming. The five of them dove over waves, racing each other.

C.J. could understand their enthusiasm. There was nothing she liked better than being in the ocean. Of course, she'd rather be swimming for pleasure than diving in to save somebody. But being a lifeguard was her job, and she was devoted to it.

She quickly inspected her tower for any earthquake damage. She didn't care what Mitch said—any earthquake above a three was serious, as far as she was concerned. She would bet that he had woken up. He was probably just too tough to admit it.

She ran her hands along the wood of the tower, checking for loose bolts and cracks. To her relief, everything seemed to be perfectly in place.

She climbed up on the tower and assumed her post. Scanning the ocean with binoculars, she spotted the eager group of swimmers. In their rush to outdo each other, they'd gone out too far.

She grabbed the bullhorn from its hook beside her. "The five swimmers away from the beach!" she called. "Turn north or south! Swim parallel to the shore! Do not move away from the beach!"

She put down the bullhorn and checked on the swimmers again with her binoculars. Either they hadn't heard her, or they didn't care how far out they were heading.

But C.J. knew that only the strongest swimmers in the world could swim for long against such a powerful current. At Baywatch, people like those five in the water right now were known as "one-way swimmers." That meant they could swim out far, but they wouldn't have the strength to make it back to shore. Even C.J. herself couldn't go out that far without a surfboard.

She turned toward Matt, who was at the next tower. "Matt, I need backup!" she shouted through the bullhorn.

Then, tossing the bullhorn aside, she grabbed her orange rescue can and ran down the ramp from her tower to the beach. She sprinted toward a bright yellow Baywatch Wave Runner at the shoreline. Pushing it into the water, she jumped on and revved the engine, driving the vehicle forward.

C.J. hurtled over the waves straight toward the swimmers.

"Help! Help me!" a woman called to her,

struggling to stay afloat. "Help me, please!"

C.J. hoped Matt was right behind her. One of the men looked as if he was starting to sink under the surface. She couldn't save all five swimmers on her own!

CHAPTER THREE

C.J. bounced across the ocean on the Wave Runner. Now all five swimmers were waving at her, calling for help.

"Help is coming! You'll be okay!" she shouted to the first woman she passed. The woman seemed strong enough to last until Matt reached her.

She glanced behind her. Matt was paddling straight toward the group on a rescue board. He was moving fast—C.J. hoped it was fast enough.

She pulled up to a man and a woman in the water. They were struggling to tread water and stay afloat.

"Here, take my hand," she told the woman. Slowly, she pulled her up onto the Wave Runner.

The woman coughed up water. "Oh," she gasped, coughing again.

"You can make it," C.J. told her.

Then she turned to the man in the water

beside them. "Grab onto the stern," she instructed him. *Two rescues down, three to go,* she thought anxiously. She turned around again, checking Matt's progress on the rescue board. He still hadn't reached a victim, but he was very close.

Just then, Logan came speeding out from around the jetty in a Rubber Ducky. It was a light but powerful Australian speedboat with two pontoons. Logan was a lifeguard from Australia who had come to Baywatch on an exchange program. He'd only been at Bay-watch for a few days, but already he'd bragged to C.J. at least three times about how superior the Rubber Ducky was to an American rescue craft.

Let's see if he's right, she thought grimly as the bright orange boat sped toward her. *I sure hope he is!* With two victims hanging onto the Wave Runner, C.J. couldn't move until she got some more backup. She knew a Scarab would be on the way any second.

Matt sat up on the rescue board and waved at Logan as he sped across the water. "Hey, Logan! Get the victim closest to you!" Matt pointed. "The male victim over there!"

Logan looked right at Matt. But instead of following Matt's directions, he went right past the male victim. The wake created by the Rub–

ber Ducky sent the water swirling even higher around the victim's head, nearly submerging him!

C.J. watched as Matt, frustrated, smacked the water with his hands. Then he lay back down and plowed forward on his rescue board, trying to reach the male victim himself.

Logan pulled up beside the female victim. Grabbing her hands, he lifted her into the Rubber Ducky. "It's okay," he told her. "I've got you." From what C.J. could see, the woman was almost lifeless.

From around the pier, a yellow rescue Scarab bounded toward the group. "That boat will carry you both to shore," she told the man and woman below her. "You're going to be fine."

"Help!" the male victim Logan had passed called out as Matt neared him.

Matt paddled up to him, sitting up and straddling the board. "Climb on!" Matt told him. "Grasp the strap, and I'll pull you up with your leg!"

The man struggled onto the board, and Matt made sure he was balanced.

That's four rescues, C.J. thought, frowning. *Now, what about the fifth?*

Just then, Newman, another member of the Baywatch team, leapt from the speeding

Scarab into the water, right beside the fifth victim. It was the third female swimmer, who was flailing her arms in the water and going under. Newman's rescue can flew out behind him as he dove into the water.

Within seconds he reached the woman and pushed the rescue can onto her chest to support her. She clutched it desperately, resting her chin on top of it and gasping for air.

That's everyone! C.J. sighed in relief. Then she remembered the victim Logan had rescued. She hoped the woman was going to be okay!

Logan jumped out of the Rubber Ducky in waist-deep water, then lifted the female victim in his arms and carried her onto the beach. He laid her on her back and leaned over her mouth, listening for a breath. Nothing. She needed mouth-to-mouth resuscitation. He held her nose closed and started breathing into her lungs.

Behind him, Matt came out of the water, helping the male victim he'd rescued. "Are you all right?" he asked. The man nodded. "Wait here."

Matt sprinted up to Logan. "Let me take over!" he said, wrestling Logan's arms away from the female victim.

"She needs CPR—do compressions!" Logan said, shrugging off Matt's grip.

Matt kneeled in the sand at the woman's waist. He ran his fingers down her rib cage, trying to find the right position. It was crucial when doing CPR. He located her sternum and started pumping the heel of his hand against it, leaning over the woman's body to create enough pressure. "One…two…three…four…five!" he counted off each compression.

He paused, and Logan breathed into the woman's mouth.

"One, two, three, four, five!" Matt chanted more urgently this time, trying to get her heart to start beating.

Logan blew more oxygen into the woman's lungs. Still no response. Far off down the beach, Logan could hear sirens—the para-medics were on the way. But if he and Matt couldn't get the woman's heart going, it might be too late.

They repeated the compressions again and again. Each time, the fear of losing the victim grew even stronger in Logan's chest.

Finally, on the sixth try, the woman coughed, spurting water out of her mouth.

"Yes!" Logan cried triumphantly, holding up her head and smiling at her. "You're going to be okay," he told her, smoothing her wet hair back from where it was plastered to her cheek.

The paramedics pulled up in a truck beside them.

"Get the oxygen!" Matt called to one of the paramedics. "You're going to be all right, ma'am." She coughed again and struggled to breathe normally as the paramedic held the oxygen mask firmly over her mouth.

Logan grinned. There was nothing more rewarding than the feeling of just having saved someone's life. He pushed a shock of his shaggy, wet, blond hair off his forehead as he watched the woman gradually revive. And on top of everything, she was kind of cute, too. He hadn't even noticed until just now, but still...

"Can I talk to you for a minute?" Matt asked, looking up at Logan.

Logan shrugged. "Sure. What about?"

"Come on." Matt took a few steps away from the paramedics' truck, so they would be out of hearing. He looked Logan squarely in the face. "What do you think you were doing out there?" he demanded.

"Um...let's see." Logan tapped his chin with his finger and gazed up at the sky. "What was I doing? Oh, yeah. Saving lives?" Logan replied calmly. He sounded almost snooty about it.

"You call that saving lives? Nearly running

one victim down to save another—just because she's female?" Matt asked. "That's incredibly stupid—not to mention dangerous. What, did you think you'd get a date out of it or something?"

Logan fixed Matt with a steely gaze. "First, *don't* tell me how to do my job. She needed help more than he did. And second, I knew me and my Rubber Ducky would get her to shore *way* before you."

"So," Matt sneered, "you and your little Rubber Ducky almost drowned that guy in your wake! Or didn't you notice?"

Logan shrugged. "Oh, but I knew you'd come to his rescue, Matt. After all, *you're* the Los Angeles ocean lifeguard," he said in a sarcastic tone. "I only *strive* to be as good as you..."

"You should," Matt said. "Because from what I can see, your skills need some major improvements!" He took a step toward Logan, who took an equal step toward him, and the two of them stared at each other. Then Matt reached out to shove Logan away just as Logan took a swing at his face.

"Hey, hey, hey! That's enough!" C.J. called, striding up and pushing them apart. "You're on duty, both of you. Please try to act like professionals."

"He's no professional," Matt corrected her.

Logan smiled at C.J. "Matt's just jealous. I beat him to the rescue, that's all. He didn't get all the hero worship he was looking for."

"Why, you lying—"

C.J. grabbed Matt's arm before he could punch Logan. "Matt, go to my tower and fill out rescue cards. *Now.*"

Matt didn't move. "I'll go after he does."

"What is this, Macho Overload Day?" Throwing up her hands in frustration, C.J. turned to Logan. "We don't compete to save lives here, Logan. We work together as a team. Your flashy tactics may have worked in Australia, but they don't have a place on our beach."

Logan frowned, his tanned face turning slightly red. "Whatever," he said in a casual tone.

"Now take your little Rubber Ducky out *slowly* past the wave line, and patrol the other side of the pier," C.J. told him firmly.

"Sure thing. See you later." He grinned at C.J., giving her a long look. Then he turned and walked away.

"I don't care if he was the top lifeguard in Australia," Matt seethed, glaring at Logan as he crashed over a huge wave in the Rubber Ducky. Logan wasn't going slowly at all. "I'm

24

not going to put up with that guy!"

C.J. would never admit it, but she felt exactly the same way about Logan. Still, they all had to work together, whether they were friends or not. "Matt, you can't let personal problems get in the way of being a good lifeguard," she said.

"I won't," Matt said. "I promise. I'd just… rather ship him back to Australia, that's all."

The way Logan was acting, C.J. thought as she headed back up onto her lifeguard tower, Matt just might get his wish.

CHAPTER FOUR

Mitch jogged along the beach at sundown, trying to collect his thoughts. Staring at the empty lifeguard towers stretched along the sand in front of him, Mitch didn't know what he could say to Hobie to change his mind about being a Junior Lifeguard. But he had to say something.

Mitch glanced toward his friend Jackie Quinn's restaurant, Jackie's Summer Place, as he started up the incline toward the board-walk. Jackie was sweeping sand away from the deck. She had just sold the restaurant and she was going to be moving soon. Mitch would be sorry to see her leave town. Besides being good friends, they'd dated for a while.

Mitch walked toward Jackie, smiling. "Hey, Jackie!" He lifted his sunglasses off his face.

"Hello, Mitch." She looked at him and smiled back. She was wearing a Hawaiian print blouse, faded jeans, and white sneakers. With her long blond hair and deep green eyes, she looked as beautiful as she had the day Mitch met her.

"Don't tell me"—Mitch stepped forward and kissed her lightly on the cheek—"you came all the way back here just to sweep up!"

Jackie shrugged, resting her chin on the tip of the broom. "Force of habit, I guess. I just want the place to look good for the new owners."

"Do you know what they're planning to turn the place into?" Mitch asked.

Jackie grinned. "That'll be your problem, not mine. By the time it opens on Memorial Day, I'll be halfway home to Pittsburgh, towing my trailer behind me."

"What about Summer?" Mitch asked. Jackie's daughter had been a guard at Baywatch for a few years.

"She flew back already," Jackie said. "I think, you know, breaking up with Matt and leaving the beach...that was about all she could handle. She wasn't up for a cross-country move, that's for sure. But she's enrolling at Penn State."

"Great!" Mitch said enthusiastically. He was glad Summer had found something she wanted to do. "So when do you leave?"

"Tomorrow morning," Jackie said. "Crack of dawn."

"Okay, then. If you want, I'll come by tonight and help you hitch up the trailer," Mitch offered.

"Mitch, you are about the sweetest man I have ever met." Jackie leaned the broom against the deck railing and reached out to give Mitch a hug. "But…"

Mitch frowned, releasing her. "There's always a but."

"Not always," Jackie said. "It's just that I think I need to be alone tonight. I want to spend my last night here looking at the ocean, and wake up to one last California sunrise." She laughed. "Then I'm getting out of town as fast as I can, before the big one hits!"

"The big one? You mean an earthquake?" Mitch scoffed. "Yeah, right. C.J. asked if I felt that tiny tremor this morning. I told her any-thing below a six is a joke."

"All I know is, Pittsburgh's earthquake–free," Jackie said. "And that's the way I want it."

"But where's the thrill? The constant excite-ment?" Mitch teased.

"Oh, I think I can live without all that," Jackie said, laughing. "Dull and boring sounds just fine right now."

Mitch frowned. It was slowly dawning on him that he probably wouldn't see Jackie again…at least not for a long time. He was truly going to miss hanging out with her, just talking and laughing. He cleared his throat and took Jackie's face in his hands. "Everyone here's going to miss you. You know that, right?"

Jackie nodded, her eyes filled with tears. "And I'm going to miss you guys, too. Especially you and Hobie. It's really been fun watching him grow up."

"Easy for you to say!" Mitch joked. *"You're* leaving town. *I'm* stuck here with a rock-and-roll radical who wants to carve his surfboard into a guitar. Or maybe he's already turned it into a keyboard, I'm not sure. All I know is, he's suddenly dead set against being a lifeguard."

Jackie gazed out at the ocean, the breeze ruffling her hair. "Kids change, Mitch. Overnight. But if singing is Hobie's dream, you have to let him chase it."

Sure, Mitch thought. *But how far?*

"Okay! Turn your heads sideways! Everyone smile!" Hobie directed his friends.

The bright light flashed in Hobie's eyes, making him see spots.

"Okay, change places!" he said, shoving his friends around the tiny photo booth on the Santa Monica pier. "One more!" The camera flashed for the fourth time, and everyone stepped out of the cramped booth.

"These are going to be so awesome," Conner said excitedly.

Hobie, J.B., Conner, and Samantha all crouched around the outside of the photo booth, eagerly waiting for the strip of photos to drop out of the machine.

"Here they come," J.B. announced, as the very end of the strip appeared.

Hobie heard the machine cut the strip of photos. As soon as it dropped into the little cup, he reached out and grabbed it before anyone else could. "Got 'em!" he cried.

"Let me see!" Samantha said.

"Hand them over, dude!" Conner shouted.

Hobie held the photos away from everyone, trying to get the first look at them. He walked a few steps back from the machine. When his friends crowded around him, he took off, jogging to the end of the pier.

J.B., Conner, and Samantha were right behind him. "Come on, Buchannon!" J.B. cried. "This is totally unfair!"

"Just let me look at them first," Hobie said, squinting to see the black–and–white photos in the early evening light.

"Hand them over!" Conner demanded, reaching for the photo strip.

Hobie lifted his hand high in the air. J.B. tugged at his sleeve, and Hobie lost his grip. The two of them watched in dismay as the wind picked up the photo strip and blew it off the end of the pier, where it drifted down onto the wet sand below.

"Oh, thanks a lot!" Hobie said, watching it flutter into the water. "You knocked the photos out of my hand!"

"Why did you grab them in the first place?" Samantha demanded.

"Yeah, you're the one who dropped them!" J.B. said.

"I didn't drop them!" Hobie insisted.

"Just go get them," J.B. said.

"Fine!" Hobie threw up his hands. He hated arguing. His parents had fought constantly before their divorce. And arguing never solved anything. "Okay, I'll get them," he said, heading for the stairs.

Down on the beach, Hobie trudged through the wet sand. He didn't see the photos anywhere. A wave splashed over his feet. They'd probably already washed away. *There goes our $1.50!* Hobie thought.

"Hey, Hobie!"

Hobie looked up and saw his friends standing on the boardwalk. "Yeah?" he called.

"Some bum got our pictures," J.B. said.

"Yeah. We saw him when you were going down there," Conner added. "He went under the pier, but he didn't come out the other side. Go get them!"

"From a bum?" Hobie asked, looking up at his friends. "Under the pier?" *Why me? Why do I always get stuck doing this stuff?* The last thing he wanted to do was ask some strange guy for his pictures. But he didn't have much choice. He took a deep breath and headed under the darkened pier.

Shafts of light filtered through the wooden slats, giving everything a slightly creepy look. Water swirled around the pilings. The tide was coming in, Hobie realized. "Hello?" he called out. Turning around, Hobie spotted some big cardboard boxes and piles of clothing—it looked as if somebody might be living down here. At Baywatch, places like this were called "sandominiums."

"Hello?" Hobie called out again. "Anybody here? Um...did anyone find some pictures on the beach?"

Suddenly, a prosthetic arm shot out in front of Hobie's face, holding the photo strip in its metal fingers. Hobie jumped back, startled. Then a man's rugged face peered out from behind a piling.

"These the snapshots you're looking for?"

the man asked, stepping out. He had a beard, a ruddy complexion, and he was wearing an old flannel shirt and a torn-up pair of blue jeans. He was barefoot.

"Um, yes," Hobie replied. He pointed at the photos, his hand shaking a little. "That's me, there, and those are my friends."

The man nodded slowly. "It's very important to have friends. Pictures of friends are actually better than the friends, because then you know you have them, but they don't get in the way," he said.

Hobie stared at him, trying to understand. He felt as if he'd just been given a really hard word problem in algebra.

"My name's Garrick," the man went on, grinning at Hobie's puzzled reaction. "What's yours?"

"Hobie."

"Hobie? Hobie like the cat, or Hobie like the surfboard?" Garrick asked.

"The surfboard. My dad used to have one." Hobie cleared his throat. "Actually, he's, you know, *waiting* for me, right out there, so if I can please have my pictures back..." He hesitated, looking at Garrick's arm as Garrick held the pictures closer to his face. Hobie reached out and took hold of the thin strip of photographs, but Garrick didn't let go of it.

"Here, press my elbow," Garrick said, as if it were a dare. "Press it right there. Go ahead."

Hobie hesitated again. He was curious to see how the arm worked, but he didn't want to offend Garrick. He looked up at the man, who nodded. Hobie pressed the elbow gently.

Garrick made a buzzing sound as the tongs holding the photos opened and the pictures dropped into Hobie's waiting hand. He laughed.

Hobie thought the whole thing was kind of cool. Weird, but cool. Garrick might be a little strange or even obnoxious, but he seemed okay. "Thanks," Hobie said.

"Sure thing. Hey, next time you're in the neighborhood, stop by and say hi. That's my place, right there. The second box, left of the central pillar." Garrick pointed to a large, empty cardboard box. "Great view, huh?" he joked.

Hobie shrugged, not sure what to say. He hated thinking that anyone had to live under the pier.

"Well, see you, kid." Garrick pressed his elbow, closing the tongs on his prosthetic arm.

"Yeah, see you," Hobie said.

Garrick turned and walked away.

Hobie watched the man go. He was almost glad the pictures had fluttered down here, just so he could meet him.

Then he glanced down at the photos. Finally he could get a decent look at them. He really *did* look like a rock star! Samantha, J.B., and Conner were going to be so psyched—the four of them looked like a real band!

And this is only the first step, Hobie reminded himself. *Tonight we lay down a few tracks on our demo tape. And then…instant fame!*

At dusk, Jackie parked her four-door car at the pull-off just above Paradise Cove. As she got out and closed the door, a piece of rust fluttered onto the ground.

She smiled, feeling a bit sad. Mitch had always called her car "Carosaurus," because it was old, rusted-out, and about as big as a Baywatch rescue boat. "This thing ought to be extinct," he'd teased her. "Hey, it got me here from Pittsburgh and it'll get me back," she'd told him more than once.

Paradise Cove had always been one of Jackie's favorite places to come to think, read, or just hang out, gazing at the gorgeous ocean below.

She took a folding beach chair out of the small trailer she was towing. The trailer was jammed with boxes and boxes of her belongings—clothes, books, pots and pans. There was even a can of sand she'd taken from the beach. She'd thought about shipping some of the stuff back home to Pittsburgh. But what was the point when she could move it herself, for free? Of course, that did only leave her enough room to sleep in—and not much else.

Jackie unfolded the chair at the edge of the cliff and sat in it. Down below, waves broke onto the jagged rocks that jutted out of the water.

She tucked her legs up, resting her chin on top of one of her knees. She stared wistfully at the Santa Monica coastline and let out a deep sigh. "I'm gonna miss this place," she told her-self softly. She couldn't help remembering all the great times—and even the sad times—she'd shared with Mitch.

But she had to move on with her life, even if it meant leaving California and all the peo-ple she loved there behind.

But that's not until tomorrow, she reminded herself. *Right now, I'm just going to sit here and enjoy this.*

She wanted to gaze at the beautiful coast until it was permanently imprinted in her memory. That way, she'd never forget Bay-watch.

CHAPTER FIVE

C.J. pulled the bright yellow note that said KNOCK BEFORE ENTERING off her apartment's front door and knocked. As soon as her room-mate, Stephanie, appeared, C.J. waved the note in front of her face. "Was this really, absolutely necessary?" she asked. C.J. had just gotten home after a long bike ride, and she was dying to take a shower and change. The last thing she wanted was to have to knock to get into her own apartment!

"Yes. Riley and I are working," Stephanie replied in an irritated voice. She had come out into the hallway to talk with C.J. before letting her even step inside the apartment. "He's the oceanographer I'm going out with tomorrow."

"Going out with?" C.J. asked. This sounded interesting. "As in..."

"As in going *out* to the Malibu fault line, to plant a seismometer. We're going over the game plan tonight," Stephanie explained.

"Well, if you're just *working* together, then

why are so worried about me barging in and spoiling your evening?" C.J. asked.

"Because you never know when a working relationship might sort of...spontaneously turn into something else," Stephanie said.

"Uh–huh." C.J. nodded. "So what am I supposed to do?"

"That's easy. Just come in, say, 'Hi, nice to meet you' and 'Good night.' Don't do anything distracting," Stephanie said.

"In other words, go to my room," C.J. said.

Stephanie nodded. "Yes. And the quicker, the better. We'd really like our privacy."

"Fine!" C.J. sighed loudly and pushed her bicycle into the apartment behind Stephanie. She was beginning to wonder about this whole roommate thing. How spontaneous was a note on the door, anyway?

"Riley, this is C.J.," Stephanie said as a man stood up from the couch. He was cute, C.J. decided, in a rugged kind of way.

"Hi," she said.

He took a step toward her and grinned. "You must be Stephanie's roommate."

"Yes, I am—" C.J. began.

Stephanie shot C.J. a warning look.

"Nice to meet you," C.J. quickly added. "Good night!" She hurried into her room, and Stephanie closed the door firmly behind her.

"So...where were we?" Stephanie asked Riley, walking back toward him. "I think you were showing me breathing techniques for free-diving." She took Riley's hand and leaned back against him, placing his hand over her stomach. "Now what was that pattern again? Two breaths in and five out?"

"No, it's two in and four out," Riley said. "Ready?"

"Mm–hm." Stephanie nodded.

"Inhale," Riley instructed. "One, two…"

Stephanie focused on controlling her breathing, as much as was possible with Riley so close to her!

"You can run," Hobie sang, playing the keyboard. "You can run!" He listened to Conner beside him, playing bass. Behind Hobie, J.B. was on drums—and on the other side of him, Samantha played electric guitar.

It was kind of hard to feel like a real band when the drummer sat next to a washer and dryer, Hobie thought, glancing over his shoulder. Maybe that was why they sounded so terrible tonight! The beat was definitely off. In fact everything sounded out of tune, even his own voice!

Hobie banged his fists against the keys. "No! Guys, come on! This is *not* working," he complained into the microphone. "At *all.*"

"Our timing's off," Samantha said, glaring at Conner. She pulled the strap of her electric guitar over her head and rested the guitar beside an amplifier.

"Hey, don't look at me! Hobie keeps falling behind," Conner said.

"That's only because J.B.'s playing behind the beat!" Hobie argued.

"You want a faster beat?" J.B. started drilling the drums, playing so fast that his hands were a blur as he went from drum to cymbal to cymbal to drum. Hobie had to admit J.B. could be good when he wanted to be. He looked like someone doing a solo at a big concert.

Then Hobie heard another crashing noise—a rumbling that couldn't be coming from the drums. It was underground!

"Earthquake!" he shouted.

J.B. stopped playing and the four of them stood staring at each other as the rumble grew louder and louder. The overhead lights swung back and forth. A basket of laundry fell off the dryer as a box of detergent crashed off a small shelf onto the floor.

In the rafters above them, stacks of boxes and crates teetered, threatening to fall. A large, heavy boat engine shifted slightly, stopping short of falling onto the concrete below.

Hobie's heart pounded in his throat. He hated earthquakes—even little ones like this! First that morning, then now...when were they going to stop?

"Excuse me. I just came out to get a flashlight." C.J. waved nervously to Stephanie and Riley, who were in the middle of a slow dance. Romantic music was playing on the stereo. "Ignore me. Keep dancing." C.J. tiptoed over to the kitchen and pulled open a drawer.

Stephanie cleared her throat loudly. "Ahem. C.J.? Why do you need a flashlight all of a sudden?" She stared disapprovingly at C.J.'s skimpy nightgown.

"You know, in case there's another quake," C.J. said, shrugging. She held up the emer-gency kit. "Okay, so I'll be going now."

Stephanie glared at her. "Go ahead."

Some people are so rude! C.J. thought. She was on her way back to her bedroom when there was a knock at the door.

"I'll get it," Stephanie grumbled.

C.J. could tell that her roommate wasn't very happy about having her "work" with Riley interrupted yet again. C.J. paused before going into her bedroom, curious to see who had knocked.

Stephanie sighed and pulled open the door.

Her younger sister, Caroline, was standing in the hall, looking as if she'd just lost her best friend. She had a small duffel bag over her shoulder. She was wearing a black denim jacket over a sundress, and her long brown hair fanned out over the collar. "Hi," she said shyly.

"Caroline?" Stephanie said.

"Oh, Steph." Caroline almost fell into her sister's arms, clinging to her in a tight hug.

"Caroline, what's wrong?" Stephanie asked, concerned.

Caroline looked over her sister's shoulder. It was only then that she seemed to notice Riley standing there. "Oh. Gosh, I'm sorry. This is a bad time."

C.J. rushed out of the bedroom doorway. "Caroline, what's going on?"

"Frank and I are getting a divorce," Caroline announced, her shoulders slumping.

C.J. gathered her friend in a hug. "Everything's going to be fine," she told Caroline.

Behind them, Riley started getting his things together, preparing to leave. Stephanie went over to him. "Hey, look, it's getting really late," he said. "We've got an early start tomorrow. Get some sleep." He leaned over to kiss her on the cheek.

"I'll try," Stephanie said.

"I really enjoyed tonight," Riley said, still holding on to her.

"Me too," Stephanie said. "See you tomorrow morning at three."

Riley headed for the door. "C.J., it was a real pleasure meeting you." He shook her hand briefly. "Caroline, I hope things work out for you."

"Thanks." She blushed as Riley went past her and out the door. "Well, that guy seemed really nice. Who was he?" Caroline asked as Stephanie led her to the couch.

"Forget about him. He and your sister have a...working relationship," C.J. said. "As in, they're *working* on one."

"We're trying to, anyway." Stephanie frowned at C.J. "Caroline, what happened this time?" she asked, sitting on the couch beside her sister.

Caroline sighed. "Frank cheated on me again. Only this time, I had the guts to leave him."

"Good for you," C.J. said encouragingly.

"So I was kind of hoping I could stay here with you guys for a little while, until I find a place of my own. Is that okay?" Caroline asked.

"Sure!" C.J. said immediately.

"Of course you can." Stephanie hugged her

sister again tightly. She was glad Caroline knew she could always come to her when she had nowhere else to go. That's what sisters were for!

"Okay, let's take it again. But this time, let's do it like we're on MTV. Ready?" Hobie asked his band.

J.B. nodded and drummed out the opening beat to their latest song.

Hobie was standing in front of the microphone in the dim, musty garage, playing the keyboard. But his mind was a million miles away. He could see it all now...he would direct his own video, and get it just the way he wanted.

The video would open with Hobie walking somewhere, wearing baggy jeans, a big T-shirt, and a baseball cap. He'd be walking along, when suddenly six or seven gorgeous girls would jog by, heading straight for him.

"You can run, you can hide, you can cheat, you can lie, but you can't get away from me..." he'd sing to them.

He'd float down a river in a boat, and the girls would be up on a bridge, trying to catch him. He'd wave back—very cool and casual, of course—and they'd run to the other side of the bridge.

Then the camera would switch—he'd be up on the bridge *with* them. He'd be running as fast as he could, and all the girls would be chasing him. The way it *should* be, he thought with a grin, picturing the girls in hot pursuit.

"Hobie! Hobie!" they'd call to him. He'd just keep running, tempting them to chase him even more. And the whole time he'd be singing and dancing, putting on his best moves—

"Hobie! Hobie!"

One by one the beautiful girls disappeared. Hobie found himself back in the garage, staring straight at his father, who was calling his name. Talk about a harsh return to reality!

"Hobie, you were supposed to be home over an hour ago," Mitch said sternly, staring at his watch.

This never happens on MTV, Hobie thought, sighing. *Why does Dad have to show up and ruin everything, just when we're getting good?*

"You didn't have to come in there and drag me out like I'm some little kid!" Hobie told his dad as soon as they walked into their house fifteen minutes later.

"If you came home when you were supposed to, I wouldn't have to come looking for you!" Mitch replied.

Hobie shrugged. "We were getting into the music and we lost track of time. So sue me."

Mitch frowned as Hobie turned away and started toward the stairs. "Hobie, we need to have a talk," Mitch said. "About your music, priorities...about a lot of things." He went over and tried to put his arm around Hobie's shoulder.

Hobie pulled away. "I don't feel like talking to you right now." Angrily, he took the steps two at a time up to his bedroom. He slammed the door and fell onto his bed, staring at the poster of Pearl Jam on the ceiling. Parents just didn't understand anything!

CHAPTER SIX

At just before three in the morning on Sunday, Stephanie stood in her living room, watching Caroline sleep. Her younger sister looked so peaceful and happy. It was hard to imagine how much pain she must be feeling over finding out that Frank was cheating on her again, and deciding that she had to get a divorce.

Stephanie tiptoed over to pull up the comforter, which had slipped halfway to the floor.

"What time is it?" Caroline whispered groggily, opening her eyes.

"It's almost three in the morning," Stephanie said. "Why don't you go sleep in my bed?"

"No, I really like it here," Caroline said, rolling over. She yawned. "Hey, Steph?"

"Yeah?" Stephanie asked, brushing a strand of hair off her sister's cheek.

"Now that Summer's gone back to Pennsylvania, I was thinking. Maybe I could get back into shape, requalify during the next recheck, and take her spot at Baywatch."

Stephanie couldn't have been more stunned. Caroline—at Baywatch? "But, Caroline, you haven't been a lifeguard since high school," she reminded her sister. She didn't want to be critical, but she wasn't sure Caroline could perform at the Baywatch level anymore.

"I know," Caroline sighed, shrugging. "But those were my happiest times, Steph. I just want to be happy again."

Stephanie smiled. "You will be, sweetie. I promise." At least she hoped her sister could find happiness again. Having a job at Baywatch near her would definitely help. "Come to headquarters with C.J.," Stephanie said. "I'll meet you there around noon, when I get back from the fault, and we can talk to Mitch about it."

"Thanks. That would be great. I really love you, Sis," Caroline said sleepily.

"I love you, too, silly. Now get some sleep." Stephanie finished tucking the comforter around Caroline, then picked up her gear and headed for the door.

Hobie sat up in bed, his eyes suddenly wide open. He had the perfect ending to the song they'd been rehearsing earlier that night! Glancing at the alarm clock on his bedside table, he saw that it was only four o'clock in the morning.

"Well, all the great artists work at weird hours," he told himself. "I gotta get this on tape!"

He tossed off the covers and quickly got dressed, pulling on a sweater over his T-shirt and shorts. Then he very quietly snuck out of the house and rode his bike to the garage practice space as fast as he could. He didn't want to forget the song playing in his head before he got a chance to record it.

Wait until the guys hear this! he thought as he stepped into the garage and switched on his keyboard.

Out on the ocean, above the Malibu Fault, Stephanie stood in a small white motorboat with Riley and the two geologists. It was just after dawn, and the early morning sun bounced off the high rocks around them, casting shadows over the boat. Max and Tom, the geologists, carefully pulled a portable computer out of a box at the rear of the boat.

"Did you check the seismometer?" Riley asked, leaning forward.

"Hold on a second," Tom said, lifting the computer. "We're almost ready."

Riley was in his wetsuit, a tank of compressed air strapped to his back. He'd been set for the dive and anxious to go ever since he met Stephanie at the boat a few hours earlier.

Tom handed him the seismometer, and Riley perched on the edge of the boat.

"Good luck!" Stephanie said, smiling at him. "Not that you'll need it."

"I'll be right back," he told her with a grin. Then he slipped the regulator into his mouth, grasped the seismometer firmly, and plunged into the ocean.

Riley swam straight down, holding his flashlight out in front of him and kicking with his swim fins to propel him deeper. When he got lower, he clipped the flashlight to his arm. Then he pulled himself forward along the rocks with one hand while holding the seismometer in the other.

He reached the ocean floor quickly, then started searching for the right spot to place the instrument. He needed to get it as close to the fault as possible.

He found a small opening—a fissure—and set the seismometer down inside it. *That ought to do it*, he thought.

* * *

Back on the boat, far above Riley, Max and Tom were evaluating the computer data. Max whistled. "Those ultra–low–frequency readings are going right off the scale," he commented.

"Could be a pre–temblor vibration," Tom said, staring at the computer screen. He shot Max a worried look. "Remember what happened in Santa Cruz, before the Loma Prieta quake?"

Stephanie walked up to the two geologists, who were sitting in the front of the boat, monitoring Riley's underwater progress. "How's he doing down there? Is everything in place?" she asked.

"Well, yes…but we're getting some very unusual readings," Tom told her, examining the information on the computer screen in front of him again.

"Unusual?" Stephanie asked. "What do you mean?"

"Riley?" Max said into his radio.

"Yeah!" Riley's voice came over the speaker.

"Can you reposition that seismometer?" Max asked. "Try getting it on bedrock."

"This is it," Tom breathed.

"What is it?" Stephanie watched the computer screen anxiously. Why did Max and Tom sound so worried all of a sudden? What was going on?

"No," Max said, shaking his head in disbelief. "This can't be happening."

"What?" Stephanie demanded. "Will somebody please tell me—"

"Riley...Riley! Get out of there!" Max cried.

At almost the same instant, Stephanie heard a loud rumbling. Her heart leapt into her throat. It was an earthquake! And Riley was—

But she didn't have a second longer to think about Riley. The motorboat suddenly lurched into the air, tipped sideways, and capsized—tossing Stephanie, Max, and Tom into the churning ocean!

At six o'clock, Mitch was calmly pouring himself a bowl of cereal when the lamp above his kitchen table started shaking—first slightly, then furiously. The silverware on the kitchen table rattled, and everything around him in the cabinets shook—the glasses, plates, and pots and pans.

He stood up and looked around nervously, instantly recognizing the force of the earthquake. *This sure feels like more than a six!* he thought, trying not to panic. *It might even be worse.*

And that meant a lot of people could be in serious danger!

Hobie woke up on the floor of the garage, his head resting on an old rolled–up sleeping bag. Dust fell into his eyes, and as he came more awake, he realized why—the whole garage was shaking!

"No!" he cried in alarm, feeling the ground underneath him rumble and shake. "Not another one!"

A canoe paddle fell from the rafters above, and Hobie blocked it with his arms. Then an empty gasoline can crashed onto his head, followed by a small cardboard box. Beside him, a bicycle that had been hanging on a hook on the wall dropped to the ground. The tires bounced up and down beside Hobie's head before the bike fell over onto the concrete floor, the pedals making a horrible scraping noise.

Hobie tried to shield himself from all the falling objects. But so many things were coming at him so fast—it was impossible to move!

Then it happened. The heavy wooden shelves against the wall tipped over—and landed right on top of him!

Hobie felt a flood of pain rush through his legs. He pushed against the shelves, trying to move them. But it was no use. He was trapped!

"Help!" he cried. But there was no one to hear him. No one even knew he was there.

Jackie sat bolt upright in bed. "Oh, no!" she cried as she felt the trailer moving. "Earthquake!" The boxes stacked all around her bed shook as the trailer lurched ahead.

But the trailer can't move, Jackie thought, panicking. *I'm parked—or at least I was parked—right beside the cliff!*

She screamed in terror as the trailer continued to move forward, tossing her out of the bed. Boxes cascaded onto her head, trapping her in the corner of the trailer.

Then Jackie heard the sound of screeching metal as the car headed downward. "No!" she shrieked. The trailer was rolling off the cliff—and she was going to die!

CHAPTER SEVEN

Mitch moved instinctively to the kitchen door-way, still in shock. Bowls and mugs were crashing through his glass cabinets and the whole room was shaking. This was the big one! And Hobie might be in danger.

"Hobie!" he called, his voice coming out in a croak. He sprang forward and sprinted up the stairs. "Hobie, hold on! Don't move."

Mitch threw open the door to Hobie's bed-room. A few things had fallen off the walls, but the room basically looked okay—a mess, as usual, but okay. Mitch saw a lump in Hobie's bed and ran to wake him. How could anyone sleep through a major earthquake like that? "Hobe, you are one serious sleeper if you—"

He shook his son. "Hey, Hob—"

But it wasn't Hobie at all. It was a pillow. Mitch felt panic rise inside him once again. He knew that he and Hobie had argued the night before, but he hadn't really expected Hobie to sneak out of the house.

If Hobie wasn't at home in bed, where was he? And was he safe?

Mitch had to find him, as soon as possible! For all he knew, Hobie was in serious danger!

Calm down and think, Buchannon, he ordered himself. *If you were Hobie, where would you have gone last night?*

When Stephanie surfaced and gazed back at the overturned boat, she couldn't believe her eyes. The waves around her were so huge, the boat had flipped upside down—and all their belongings were floating in the water around them.

Spotting Max beside her, she grabbed him around the neck and started swimming, guiding him back to the boat. They could use the capsized boat as a giant life preserver, if nothing else.

She pushed Max up against the boat. "Hold on," she told him, pressing his hands onto the outer rim of the boat. "I've got to get Tom."

"D–don't leave me!" Max pleaded, desperation in his voice.

Stephanie turned around. Her eyes widened. Tom had already slipped under! She took a deep breath and dove down to find him. She wouldn't have much time.

*   *   *

Hobie tossed an empty, dirty cardboard box off his face and struggled to free himself from the pile of junk on top of him, especially the heavy wooden shelves.

"Hel–lo!" he called. "Is anybody out there?"

He pushed in vain at the heavy boards, unable to move them. His legs felt as if they'd been crushed, though he figured he'd probably only end up with some very serious bruises. "Hey, I'm stuck! Hello!"

The only response was a creaking from the rafters above. Hobie looked up and found himself staring right at the huge boat engine. The rafters it had been stored on were cracked nearly in two. The boat engine was perched precariously on the broken part. The rafters wouldn't be able to bear its weight for much longer.

"Oh, no," Hobie moaned, staring up at the engine. He tried to will it to stay put just by looking at it.

Suddenly, there was another aftershock, and the rafters came apart a bit more. The boat engine shifted slightly.

With the shelves on his legs, Hobie couldn't move. But if he didn't get out soon, that engine was going to fall directly onto him.

Please, he thought wildly. *Somebody please find me here—soon!*

* * *

"Max!" Stephanie gasped, swimming back to the boat with Tom cradled under her arm. "You'll have to hold him!"

"I can't," Max protested.

"Just do it," Stephanie ordered him. She pushed Tom toward Max, resting his neck on the boat. She pinched his nose closed and started giving the geologist mouth–to–mouth resuscitation.

Luckily, it didn't take long for Tom to come around. Within seconds he was conscious, though very weak.

"What about Riley?" Max asked anxiously, holding Tom's body against the capsized boat with his left arm.

Stephanie looked across Tom at Max. "How close to the fault was he?"

"*Close?* He was *in* it!" Max told her.

Stephanie felt her legs turn to rubber. In the fault...during a massive earthquake? That meant Riley was probably seriously hurt. Possibly even...dead.

She had to get down there to find him—and save him if she could!

Riley pushed at one of the giant rocks that had fallen into the fissure when he was placing the seismometer. He couldn't move it at all—or any of the other rocks blocking him in, either. He was stuck. And there was no getting out—at least not by himself.

I guess I ought to feel lucky–I'm still alive, he told himself.

But maybe not for long.

It had all happened so fast. The memory of the earthquake was already becoming a blur in his mind. He'd just found the perfect spot for the seismometer and put it down on bedrock, just as Max asked.

And then it was as if the ocean floor had opened up beneath him. The intense under-ground rumbling had only lasted a few sec-onds, but it seemed to go on forever. The violent water pressure had heaved rocks all around him. Then the world had tilted side-ways, destroying Riley's sense of equilibrium.

He knew he was very lucky not to have been hit on the head and knocked uncon-scious by one of the falling rocks. But he also knew that he'd need even more luck to get out of there alive.

Stephanie knows I'm down here. So do Max and Tom. Help is probably already on its way, he decided. As frustrating as waiting would be, he'd just have to hang tight until they showed up.

He hoped there weren't any serious after-shocks. He was in enough danger already—if a rock fell and blocked the fissure completely, nobody would even be able to find him.

"Hobie! Hobie?" Mitch forced the door open and stepped into the cluttered garage. The place was a complete disaster area!

"I'm here, Dad," Hobie said, his voice hoarse with fear and relief. "Hurry!"

Mitch pushed debris out of his way, trying to get to Hobie. "Are you all right?"

"I don't know," Hobie said. "I can't move my legs. I'm stuck! Hurry, Dad. That thing up there is gonna fall!"

Mitch looked anxiously up at the boat engine straining against the fractured wood rafters. There was no way the wood would support it much longer. And if that massive engine fell, there would be no hope for Hobie.

"Hang on," Mitch said, pushing a surfboard out of the way. "Just hang on." He used all of his strength to lift the heavy wooden shelving unit off Hobie's legs. As he lifted, he kept his eyes on the boat engine. *Don't fall!* he commanded the engine silently. *Don't you dare fall!*

"Hang on, pal," he told Hobie, still struggling with the shelves that were lying across his son's legs. They were even heavier than he'd thought.

**Hobie is
ready
for surfing
action!**

**Aussie lifeguard Logan and Hobie
prepare for the next rescue mission.**

Mitch checks out the turbulent ocean as another aftershock threatens to strike.

Matt and C.J. spot a group of swimmers in danger.

Baywatch lifeguard Matt Brody.

C.J. settles an argument between Matt and Logan.

Stephanie and Caroline Holden— two very different sisters with the same passion: saving lives.

C.J. and Matt share a quiet moment.

Hobie is torn between his desire to leave California and his loyalty to his dad.

The Baywatch team prepares for a water rescue!

Stephanie responds to an emergency call.

The Baywatch team saves a geology crew from disaster!

**Mitch and C.J.
caught off-guard.**

**C.J., Matt, Stephanie, and Caroline
take time out for fun.**

On board with the Baywatch crew.

**Hobie and his dad
celebrate a job well done!**

Just then, the rafters above them creaked. "Dad! It's going to fall!" Hobie cried.

The engine moved again—and it began to plummet toward them!

CHAPTER EIGHT

"Slide out!" Mitch yelled to Hobie. With a final desperate burst of strength, he raised the shelving unit off Hobie's legs.

Frantically, Hobie slithered across the floor as fast as he could. Mitch grabbed Hobie's hand and pulled him to his feet.

"Look out!" Hobie yelled, just as the boat engine crashed to the floor. It destroyed everything underneath it, cutting the metal beach chair in half and smashing the empty gasoline can flat.

Hobie threw his arms around his dad, his heart pounding.

"You all right?" Mitch asked, clutching Hobie tightly.

Hobie didn't answer. His whole body was shaking, and he couldn't stop thinking of what had almost happened. Just two more seconds…and he would have been pulverized, like that beach chair.

"It's going to be okay," Mitch told him, patting his back. "You're okay."

C.J. stepped gingerly out of her bedroom, her legs shaking. She still couldn't believe the force of the earthquake. She'd never felt any quake that strong before. It had to have been at least a six on the Richter scale! But at least she was alive.

The apartment was a total mess. So much for all that work they'd done a few years ago to make the place "structurally sound"!

"Caroline, are you all right?" C.J. called, picking her way through the debris scattered on the floor: plants in pots that had crashed to the ground, books that had fallen out of shelves, broken vases, and shattered CD jewel cases.

"I hurt all over," Caroline moaned from the couch.

"Oh, no," C.J. said, trying to hurry over to her. "Well, do you think you can walk? Because I think we should get out of here." She lifted a blue pipe and a cracked wooden beam that had toppled onto the couch, trapping Caroline's leg. "As fast as possible!"

"I think so, too," Caroline said. She swung her legs over the edge of the couch, and struggled to stand up.

C.J. reached out to take Caroline's hands, helping her to her feet. One of Caroline's knees buckled when she tried to take her first step. "Here. Put your arm around my waist," C.J. instructed.

C.J. and Caroline had taken a few steps together through the mess on the floor when all of a sudden, the room started to shake again. Whatever was left on the walls clattered against the wood, and the windows rattled, threatening to smash at any moment.

"C.J.!" Caroline cried. Plaster crumbled to the floor, and the two of them covered their heads. "What was that?" she gasped.

"It's just an aftershock," C.J. said, trying to reassure her friend. But the truth was, she didn't feel too safe herself.

"Eek!" Caroline covered her head as more plaster suddenly rained down from the ceiling. One end of a beam broke through the ceiling and crashed down right behind them.

C.J. and Caroline raced out of the apartment, rushed down the hall to the doorway, and ran out into the early morning sunshine. As they hurried away across the parking lot, C.J. glanced over her shoulder and saw their building swaying from the aftershocks.

That was a close one, she thought, helping Caroline along the sidewalk. *Way too close!*

                    *   *   *

Logan jumped out of his yellow Baywatch rescue truck and ran to the top of a huge pile of
sand. "Let me through!" he yelled, grabbing a
shovel from another lifeguard.

He'd been on his way to lifeguard duty
when the emergency call came over the radio.
A woman and her children were trapped in a
truck directly beneath him, under the sand.
The quake had buried them alive in a landslide!

Logan couldn't imagine how it would feel to
be stuck inside a vehicle—and not be able to
see out the windows. *Those kids are probably terrified*, he thought. *And their mom's scared out of her
wits, too!*

Logan dug into the sand with the shovel,
surrounded by other Baywatch guards doing
the same thing. They furiously tossed sand
aside, trying to uncover the truck beneath. It
was impossible to know exactly where the victims were located under the massive heap of
sand.

If the people trapped inside didn't get air
soon...

That was when Logan heard it.

A yell for help—coming from right beneath
him!

"I hear something!" he shouted to the others.

                       65

"Can't you go any faster?" he exhorted them.

"Agh! Help!" A woman's screams could be heard now, faint through the thick blanket of sand.

"We've got to get her," Logan muttered. "I've got to get her out!" Just then his shovel hit something hard. "I've hit something! Here, hold this." He passed his shovel to the guy next to him and got onto his knees, digging through the sand with his hands.

He quickly uncovered the pickup truck's moonroof. "Hand me that crowbar," he said to a female guard beside him.

"Help us, please!" the woman in the truck begged, pressing her palms against the clear moonroof.

"Get down!" Logan told her. "I don't want to hurt you!"

"No," she sobbed.

"Come on, you'll be all right," Logan said calmly. "We'll get you out!" He dug at the edge of the moonroof with the crowbar. A corner came off, and he lifted the plastic off the rest of the way. "I've got it!"

The woman was gasping as she handed up her daughter, a little girl with her blond hair tied in a purple ribbon. Logan put his hands under the girl's arms and pulled her out of the truck, smiling to put her at ease. "Okay!" he said, handing her to another lifeguard. "Here we go, mates."

The woman handed up her son next, and Logan pulled him to safety, too. Then the woman herself emerged from the roof, sobbing hysterically and shaking all over.

"Thank you," she said to Logan in a trembling voice. "You saved our lives. I'm still so scared."

"It's going to be okay," Logan told her soothingly. "Don't worry."

As he helped the woman walk over to join her children, Logan heaved a huge sigh of relief. Three saves already, and he wasn't even officially on duty yet.

From what he'd seen on television before he left his apartment, this was going to be the busiest day ever for the Los Angeles lifeguards. People all over the city were suffering—freeways had cracked, houses were on fire, and there was always the threat of a tidal wave.

It's going to be some day, all right, Logan thought as he climbed back into his truck. He only hoped he'd be able to save more lives before it was all over.

Mitch rushed across the parking lot outside Baywatch headquarters. The pavement was cracked, and in one place, it had split completely in two, with one side three feet higher than the other.

This doesn't look good, Mitch thought with a frown as he headed inside. Grabbing a rescue can, he used it to knock out any remaining shards of glass in the window frames. Then he pushed over a filing cabinet that was blocking the entryway to the office. "Hello?" Mitch called out.

"We're in here!" Newman replied.

"Everybody okay?" Mitch asked.

"Yeah, we're all right," Newman said.

"Any structural damage to this place?" Mitch asked.

"We held up pretty well, considering what happened to the rest of the city," Newman told him. In the background, the TV was on, reporting damage all over the city: houses destroyed, their sides split completely in half, downed power lines, and raging fires.

"Has anyone heard from Stephanie?" Mitch asked. "She was heading out to the Malibu Fault today."

"I radioed from a unit," Newman said. "Nothing. No response."

"Stay on that, will you? We've got to reach her," Mitch said. What could have happened to a boat out on the water in such a major earthquake? Mitch didn't even want to imagine.

He knew that there would be many others in trouble, too—and that everyone at Baywatch needed to get moving as soon as possible to save them.

. "What's in our zone?" Mitch asked John, the on-duty switchboard operator.

"Pier fire in Del Rey," John replied.

"A landslide buried a car on the Pacific Coast Highway," Newman added. "We were first on scene. Four units. I sent one Scarab to back up at the pier."

Mitch nodded. "Good work," he told the guys.

"Where's Hobie?" Newman asked. "Is he okay?"

"He's on the beach, and he's pretty shook up. He says he doesn't want to go anywhere something can fall on him," Mitch said.

"I don't blame him," Newman said, glancing around the trashed office.

"You don't know the half of it," Mitch said. "Newman, I almost lost him. It was way too close."

Just then, Matt rushed into the office, pulling a white Baywatch uniform shirt on over his bare chest. "Mitch! I've got a guy with a broken leg who needs first aid downstairs!"

"I'll take care of it," Newman said quickly, heading out of the office.

"Man, the beach just opened up and *swallowed* my truck," Matt told Mitch. "I couldn't believe it."

"Believe it," Mitch said, shaking his head. "Word is that quake was a 7.2."

Matt's face fell. "Was it the big one everyone keeps talking about?"

"I don't know," Mitch said, shrugging. "But if it wasn't, then it was a foreshock and I don't want to know what's coming next. John, is the switchboard up yet?" he called over to the operator.

"Almost on–line!" John replied.

Mitch walked over to him. "Contact the Santa Monica P.D. on frequency one. Let them know we're available for emergency response. Then contact northern and southern sections to get a damage assessment."

John nodded. When the switchboard's lights lit up, he adjusted the headphones and spoke into the mike. "This is L.A. County lifeguards, Baywatch headquarters, calling S.M.P.D...."

"We're going to be busy," Mitch told Matt grimly. "Get ready."

"Is everybody all right?" C.J. asked, helping a limping Caroline up the stairs and onto the deck outside Baywatch headquarters. She was a little embarrassed to still be wearing her nightgown over a pair of jeans.

Matt looked up from the pile of glass shards he was sweeping into a dustpan. "C.J.! And Caroline?" He sounded very surprised to see Stephanie's younger sister. "You guys all right?"

Caroline ignored his question. "Has anyone heard from Stephanie?" she asked, a hint of desperation in her voice.

"Not yet," Matt said, and Caroline gasped. "But that doesn't mean anything!" Matt assured her quickly.

"Hey, C.J.!" Mitch called from inside head-quarters.

"You stay here with Matt," C.J. told Caroline. Caroline nodded, supporting herself by hold-ing onto the wooden deck railing.

"You sure picked a great time to come to L.A.," Matt said wryly, stepping closer to her.

Caroline grasped his hand. "Matt, Stephanie's at the epicenter of this whole thing. Do you think she's all right?"

Matt squeezed her hand tightly, then put his arm around her. "Don't worry, Caroline," he said. "If anyone can handle things out there, it's your sister."

CHAPTER NINE

Inside headquarters, C.J. rushed up to Mitch and threw her arms around him. "So, did you feel *that* earthquake?" she asked.

Mitch laughed slightly. "I think they felt it in Las Vegas."

Behind them, the television showed a series of photographs taken by an aerial camera. Each picture revealed a more devastating scene than the one before it. A helicopter reporter was describing the disaster that had affected so many areas of the city of Los Angeles.

The pictures made C.J. feel a little sick to her stomach. "So much destruction..." she muttered. "It's like a nightmare."

Mitch nodded, then grabbed C.J.'s shoulders tightly. "Listen, C.J., we've got to start moving. And the only way to the marina is by water. I want you and Newman to take Wave Runners. Bring two Scarabs back here. In the meantime, I'll get the land-based operation up and running. As soon as you get back, we're going after Stephanie."

C.J. nodded. "I'll hurry!" She ran back out onto the deck. Caroline made a move to follow her. "You're staying here!" C.J. said.

"But I want to go help Stephanie!" Caroline cried.

"No way! Not today!" C.J. replied, whirling around to stop Caroline in her tracks. "Matt—take care of her, okay?" Quickly heading down the stairs to grab a Wave Runner from the beach, she bumped right into Logan, who was on his way up the stairs.

"Whoa!" Logan grabbed C.J.'s arm to keep her from falling. "Careful, darling. I don't want to survive my first shaker and be sent flying downstairs by you."

"Sorry." C.J. yanked her arm out of his grasp. "I was in a hurry." She continued down the stairs, completely focused on the task ahead of her.

Logan strolled the rest of the way up the stairs and walked over to Caroline and Matt. He grinned at Matt, who was holding Caroline's trembling hands. "You know, I was wondering where you were, Matt. But I can see why you'd rather be here...instead of getting your hands dirty digging people out of landslides, like me." He smiled, gazing into Caroline's deep blue eyes. "Can't say as I blame you, mate."

Matt glared at him. "There are a lot of lives still to save this morning, pal. And this happens to be Stephanie's sister, who was hurt in C.J. and Stephanie's apartment this morning."

"Oh." Logan nodded. "Beauty runs in the family, I see. I'm Logan," he said to Caroline, extending his hand for her to shake.

"Caroline," she said, not really paying attention. Her mind was still focused on Stephanie. What if her sister was hurt? If she'd been directly over the fault when the earthquake hit...who knew what could have happened to her?

"Matt! I need you back in here!" Mitch yelled out the window.

Matt glanced at him over his shoulder and nodded. "I'll be right back," he told Caroline. Then, with a final glare at Logan, he took off and went inside headquarters.

"Hmm. He sure didn't want to let *you* go," Logan observed. "Are you his G.F.?"

"His what?" Caroline asked.

"His girlfriend," Logan explained.

Caroline shook her head. "No. Matt and I are just friends."

The smile on Logan's face widened. "I see. You know, I've only been here three days. I'm from Tasmania, and I'm still trying to learn how all the pieces fit together." He shrugged.

Caroline looked at Logan, giving him her full attention for the first time. His eyes sparkled when he smiled, and he was actually almost charming...when he wasn't being rude. *Who is this guy, anyway?* she wondered. *And what is he doing at Baywatch?*

Stephanie struggled to support Tom. He had regained consciousness, but he was too weak to hold on to the overturned boat by himself. She didn't know how much longer she could support his weight.

Beside her, Max was hanging on desperately, clinging to the edge of the boat for dear life. She knew neither one of the men could hold out forever. She was an experienced ocean swimmer, in top shape, and even she was growing more and more tired.

Tom started to shiver. The first sign of hypothermia, Stephanie realized. If he got too cold, he'd pass out—and she'd never be able to hold him up then.

"I've got to swim under the boat and get the life vests," Stephanie told Max.

"Why isn't anyone coming to get us?" he said, his teeth chattering with the cold—and fear.

75

"They'll come. They know we're here," Stephanie told him. She noticed Max's breathing was getting ragged—he was breathing much too quickly. If he kept it up, he would start hyperventilating. "Max, take some deep breaths," she said, trying to sound reassuring. "You're okay. You've got to stay calm for me. I need you to hold on to Tom while I go under the boat."

"I can't do that!" Max protested. "I'll drown!"

"You'll drown for sure if I don't get the life vests," Stephanie told him sharply. "Now hold on to him!"

Max nodded, finally seeming to grasp the reality of the situation. He moved over slightly, grabbed Tom's arm, and held it up on the bottom of the capsized boat. "Hang in there, Tom," he said.

Satisfied that the two men would be all right for the next few minutes, Stephanie dove underwater. She didn't have another second to lose. Once she got Max and Tom into life vests, she could make the most important dive of all: the one to save Riley.

Deep in the water below Stephanie, Riley pushed against the rocks that were trapping him for what felt like the hundredth time. None of them budged.

Riley estimated that he'd been stuck down there for at least an hour, but he wasn't sure. One thing he did know: his tank only had a limited supply of air, and he was beginning to run out.

Why wasn't anyone coming yet? He peered out around the largest rock on top of the fissure. Nothing. All he could see was water.

Maybe the earthquake got them, too, he thought. *And if that's true, then nobody knows where I am...and nobody's coming.*

CHAPTER TEN

When Stephanie surfaced holding two life vests, she saw Tom's head about to slip under the water. Alarmed, she swam quickly over to him and hoisted his shoulders back up on the boat.

"Sorry," Max apologized. "I tried, but I—I couldn't hold him."

"It's okay. Here. Put this on." Stephanie put the life vest around Max and helped him fasten the straps. Then she put the other life vest around Tom and pulled the straps tightly closed. She pushed Tom backward, making sure his head was above water as he floated on his back with his legs out in front of him. She'd been right to get the life vests—neither one of the geologists had the strength to hold on to the boat much longer, especially not with cold fingers.

"Oh, what's the point? We're all going to die out here anyway," Max said, looking nervously at the ocean water around him.

"No one's going to die!" Stephanie declared. "Don't even say that!"

"Riley's probably dead already," Max continued, as if she hadn't said a word.

Stephanie bit her lip. She had a horrible feeling Max was right.

Hobie stood on the beach in the warm morning sun. Only he wasn't warm. He was freezing. He couldn't seem to stop shaking.

He watched as C.J. and Newman sped toward Baywatch headquarters in two Scarabs. They couldn't come close to shore in the Scarabs. But as soon as they drew up, a team of lifeguards ran out of headquarters. Hobie figured they'd head out in the waiting Sea Raider and Logan's Rubber Ducky, which could move more quickly and smoothly in shallow water.

When the team got closer, Hobie saw that his dad, Matt, Logan, and Barnett, another member of the Baywatch crew, were the lifeguards. Stephanie's sister Caroline was limping along behind them, looking as if she wanted to go out, too.

Mitch rushed up to Hobie. "We have to go help Stephanie and some people she's with," he said. "Caroline's going to stay with you, okay? Are you all right?"

Hobie nodded. "Yeah."

"Everything's going to be fine," Mitch said. "Are you sure you're okay?"

Hobie nodded again and his father started to run off. Hobie got a sudden, terrible feeling that he was going to embark on something extremely dangerous...something that might end in disaster. "Dad?" he called out.

Mitch turned around, jogging backward. "What?"

"Get back as soon as you can," Hobie said.

Mitch gave him a salute, and for a second, Hobie felt like a little kid again. Then Mitch took off again to join the other guards in the waiting boats.

Caroline put her hand on Hobie's shoulder. She didn't say a word.

Hobie just stood there on the beach without moving, watching his dad speed away in the Sea Raider until he was no longer in sight.

Logan and Barnett rode beside Matt and Mitch in the Rubber Ducky. Logan gunned the engine, and the Rubber Ducky crashed through the waves, shooting them ahead. Once they reached C.J.'s Scarab, they climbed onto the large yellow boat.

A few seconds later, Matt and Mitch pulled up in the Sea Raider and climbed aboard the other Scarab, which was being piloted by Newman.

"John, we'll need the Rubber Ducky and the Sea Raider picked up," Newman radioed to headquarters.

"Roger," the reply came back on the radio. "Sending out swimmers."

There was a pause. Then John's voice returned, sounding more urgent.

"Mitch! I just saw something on the news! It's Jackie's trailer—and it's hanging off a cliff above Paradise Cove! The helicopter reporter said there's no rescue underway yet!"

Matt and Mitch stared at each other. "Jackie's trailer," Matt said. "How can that be—?"

"She was parked above the cove. She told me she'd be there, for her last night in California!" Mitch said. He couldn't imagine Jackie trapped in her trailer like that. Had she gotten out in time?

Then he remembered where he'd been when the earthquake hit: in the kitchen, just barely out of bed, pouring a bowl of cereal. It had been only six o'clock in the morning. Jackie probably hadn't had time to do anything.

He glanced at the other Scarab, speeding out to the Malibu Fault beside them. There was really no question of what to do.

"Matt, you and I will head up to Jackie," he announced. "Newman, you go with the others to find Stephanie—they'll need you out there."

Newman nodded and prepared to jump onto the other Scarab.

"C.J.!" Mitch shouted, straining to be heard above the boat's engines. "C.J.! Newman's coming with you! We've got another rescue! We'll meet you out there!"

C.J. nodded and pulled her rescue boat closer to theirs so Newman could jump onto it. As he leapt across, Logan waved at Matt, giving him a superior smile.

Matt glowered in return. "Yeah, have a nice trip," he muttered under his breath. "Don't forget to stop combing your hair long enough to actually rescue somebody."

"What's with you two, anyway?" Mitch asked, turning the boat toward Paradise Cove.

Matt shrugged. "Nothing. We just can't stand each other, that's all."

"Well you'd better learn how to," Mitch advised him. "We don't have time for personality conflicts on days like today. Now come on, we've got to focus on rescuing Jackie! If she's up on the cliff, we'd better change into our climbing gear."

Mitch opened one of the boat's storage compartments and pulled out two pairs of

bright yellow cotton coveralls and two hel–
mets.

Hang on, Jackie, he thought, gazing out
toward Paradise Cove. *Just hang on until we get
there!*

CHAPTER ELEVEN

Caroline sat on the beach, pushing her toes under the sand and then wiggling them through. In the distance, she saw the two bright yellow rescue boats take off, and a minute later, two lifeguards ran into the water. They were heading toward the abandoned Rubber Ducky and Sea Raider, apparently to bring the vehicles back in.

I want to be doing that, she thought. *I want to be a lifeguard again.* Her leg was already feeling a lot better.

But for the moment, she had to stay where she was, stuck on the beach. She glanced sideways at Hobie. Maybe she could get the poor kid to relax and chill out. Caroline had never seen him so shook up before. Hobie was still staring at the horizon, as if he wasn't going to let his dad out of his sight.

"So, I heard you had an exciting morning," Caroline prompted finally.

"You mean almost dying?" Hobie said

fiercely. "That was exciting all right. And I'm never going through anything like it again!"

Caroline felt a little shocked by the force of Hobie's reaction. He was taking all of this so hard! That wasn't like him.

Then again, maybe he was right to feel that way, Caroline thought. After all, until she knew Stephanie was safe and sound, Caroline was going to be pretty upset, too. Terrified, actually. But she couldn't let Hobie think that way.

"Hobie," she began. "You can't say never—"

"Yes, I can. Because I'm out of here!" Hobie declared. "I'm going to live with my mom in Ohio. That's it!"

"Your dad said the reason you almost got…hurt…this morning is because you were in that rickety old garage," Caroline pointed out. "Your house is okay. Your dad didn't get hurt, right?"

"Not this time, no," Hobie said. "But what about the next time? Look at all this destruction. We could all end up homeless, or even dead!" He turned away and stared down the beach.

"Come on, Hobie. You're just feeling emotional right now," Caroline argued. "You're probably still in shock. We all are. And once you realize—"

"That guy," Hobie said slowly, interrupting her. His mind seemed to be a million miles away. "What happened to him?"

Caroline looked down the beach, following Hobie's gaze. "What guy? I don't see anyone."

"This homeless guy I met yesterday. He lives under the pier," Hobie said.

Under the pier? Caroline thought. That didn't sound good. Right now, the pier was probably in pieces.

Mitch stared at Jackie's big rust-colored car, which was dangling off the edge of the cliff. All the way over in the boat, he had hoped against hope that the car and trailer wouldn't be hers. But it was Carosaurus, all right. And the tires looked as if they were barely touching the rocks underneath the car.

Mitch could hardly imagine how Jackie was feeling right now—if she was still inside the trailer. Maybe she'd gotten out somehow, he thought hopefully. But if she had...wouldn't she be standing nearby, watching her trailer? After all, everything she owned was inside it, all the things she was moving back to Pennsylvania.

Mitch's heart sank at the realization. Jackie had to be in that trailer. And that meant she was facing certain death, unless he and Matt could get up there and get her out before the car and the trailer crashed down the cliff onto the rocks below. It was the kind of fall that would be almost impossible to survive.

Mitch somberly handed Matt the climbing gear, and Matt started to put it on the paddleboard. The Scarab was as close to the shore as it could get. Mitch was just about to leave the boat when he heard the sound of an approaching helicopter overhead.

He glanced up at the sky, shielding his eyes from the sun. It was a news copter from one of the L.A. television stations. As it hovered above Jackie's trailer, Mitch turned to Matt. "Forget the climbing gear. I have a better idea."

Matt gave him a puzzled look, but Mitch didn't have time to explain. He started waving his arms frantically, trying to catch the helicopter pilot's attention.

"Hey! Over here!" Mitch shouted, hoping the cameraman perched on the helicopter's skids would notice him.

The helicopter circled the cliff, still hovering close to Jackie's car and trailer. Finally, the helicopter passenger—a woman wearing a headset—spotted Mitch. It was a reporter Mitch recognized from television. She turned to the pilot, and the helicopter headed closer to the Scarab.

"Lower!" Mitch shouted excitedly. If they'd only come down and pick them up, he and Matt could get to the top of the cliff to save Jackie faster than they could ever climb. "Come down!"

Matt started waving, too, gesturing with his hands for the copter to come lower.

The helicopter hovered over the Scarab. Strong wind currents created by the propellers whipped the water around Mitch and Matt, and they struggled to keep their balance.

The pilot turned the helicopter, lowering it over the boat enough so that Matt and Mitch could grab onto the skids. Mitch wrapped his arms around the skid as tightly as he could, and the helicopter headed up, lifting him and Matt high above the ocean. Mitch almost couldn't believe how fast they were moving.

Beside him, Matt slipped slightly, losing his grip as the helicopter turned in the air. But he grabbed back on, and the two of them rode safely until the helicopter reached the top of the cliff and gently set them down.

Mitch hit the ground running. He gave the thumbs-up signal to the pilot, reporter, and cameraman, and headed straight toward Jackie's trailer. Matt was right beside him. Mitch knew he'd have only a split second to evaluate the situation and make a decision.

He gazed at the trailer. If he could separate the car from the trailer, Jackie might have a chance. But that would only be the first step. He'd have to pull Jackie out of the trailer, too.

The helicopter set down on the far edge of the cliff, so it wouldn't dislodge Jackie's car and trailer with its movement.

Mitch ran back to the copter. "Do you have a harness?" he asked the pilot and reporter.

"Sure," the reporter told him, nodding as she readjusted her headset.

"Do you think you can lift me out over the hitch?" Mitch pointed to Jackie's car. "I want to separate the vehicles."

"We can give it a try," the pilot said.

Mitch pointed to Matt, who was standing off in the distance. "That's Matt over there. Watch him—he'll give you the signals!"

"Okay," the reporter said, nodding.

Mitch turned around and looked back at the trailer. It had shifted slightly even in the last few seconds, and was rocking back and forth in the wind. "Come on!" he said. "Let's do it!"

Jackie clutched a framed photograph of her and Summer tightly, her back pressed against a cardboard box. The trailer wouldn't stop shaking! It kept rocking back and forth like a seesaw. Jackie had a feeling she was hanging onto the cliff by one wheel. And that one wheel was all that was keeping her from careening down the rocks in the trailer.

Another aftershock hit the trailer. The vehicle shook back and forth even more violently, its metal creaking and whining, threatening to give way.

"No!" Jackie wailed, sobbing. "No!"

She was never going to see her daughter again! *Summer, I love you,* she told her silently, pressing the picture against her as the tears splashed down her cheeks. *Always remember that!*

CHAPTER TWELVE

Hobie sprinted down the beach as fast as he could. Caroline was right behind him, still limping slightly. Hobie couldn't believe he hadn't thought about Garrick before now. He'd been standing on the beach feeling sorry for himself for fifteen minutes already—and that whole time, Garrick might have been in danger!

Maybe he's already drowned! Hobie thought, fear gripping him as he ran to the pier where Garrick lived.

He stopped short when he reached the tall wooden pilings. Parts of the pier looked wrecked, but the damage wasn't as bad as he'd thought. But he couldn't go under there now. He couldn't go under anything that might fall on him in an aftershock. But he had to do something to see if Garrick had survived the quake.

Hobie cupped his hands around his mouth and yelled as loudly as he could. Water rushed around his knees, the waves made higher by the earthquake. "Garrick! Garrick, are you there?" Hobie shouted, the ocean drowning out his voice.

There was no answer. Hobie paced back and forth at the edge of the pier. Now what?

Caroline came up behind him. "He lives under there?" She pointed to the back of the pier.

Hobie nodded. His stomach felt as if it was tied into a hundred knots.

"Then what are we waiting for?" Caroline asked. "Let's go!" She grabbed Hobie's hand and headed underneath the pier.

Hobie jerked back, pulling his hand away. "No, I can't. You go. He lives right under there, on the left side." He stared nervously at a beam above them. It had snapped free, and it was hanging down, the wood making a horrible creaking sound. The whole thing reminded him of the garage, and how he'd been lying on the floor, looking up at the boat engine on the broken rafter.

Caroline looked at Hobie and frowned. "Okay," she said finally. "You wait here. I'll be back. Don't worry."

Hobie watched as Caroline picked her way over broken chunks of wooden piling. He had never felt like such a wimp in his whole life.

He was afraid. Really afraid. And because of that, he was letting somebody else down. Somebody who might really need him. But he still couldn't seem to move.

Just then, Caroline rushed out from under the pier. "Hobie!" she gasped, breathless. "A beam fell on him—I think he's unconscious. I can't lift the beam off by myself. I tried, but—I really need your help!" She brushed a wet strand of hair off her face.

The wooden beam above them creaked again, and Hobie had another vision of himself, lying on the garage floor, waiting and watching the rafters about to give way. The boat engine had fallen a millisecond before his dad pulled him from the wreckage. One millisecond between life and death.

"I'll go get someone," Hobie told Caroline.

"There's no time! Hobie, he could have drowned by now! Come on, hurry!" Caroline urged. She ran back under the pier.

Hobie hesitated. *Garrick could drown...and all because I'm too afraid.* He couldn't let that happen. Taking a deep breath, he ran under the pier behind Caroline. As he got closer, he saw her crouched over Garrick, giving him mouth-to-mouth resuscitation. A beam was lying across Garrick's cardboard box.

A wave came toward them, breaking just a

few feet away. Caroline covered Garrick's nose and mouth, protecting him from the rushing water. "If I can keep him alive until a high wave comes in, we can float the beam off him!" she said. She leaned over to give Garrick another breath.

Okay, Hobie told himself. *Think of what you can do to help. Think of what Dad would do.*

He wrapped his hands around the heavy beam and tried to lift it off Garrick's torso. He wasn't strong enough—it wouldn't budge. "It's too heavy!" he told Caroline, straining with all of his might.

"When a wave comes in, push!" she said, supporting Garrick's head with her hands, struggling to keep it above water.

"I can't move it," Hobie said, gritting his teeth as he pushed. The piling was about as big around as a telephone pole.

"Okay, this is it." Caroline pointed to an incoming wave, which was just beginning to break. "When it hits, push!"

"All right," Hobie said, taking a deep breath. If it took every last ounce of strength he had, he was going to do it.

The wave rolled in. "Push!" Caroline yelled.

Hobie shoved at the wooden piling—and as the wave lifted up one end, he managed to finally lift it off Garrick enough so that Caro–

line could start to pull him free.

Together they lugged Garrick off the wet sand, using the strong incoming waves to help. A few moments later, they came out from underneath the pier, and Caroline started mouth–to–mouth again, this time on dry sand, free from danger.

Hobie watched her anxiously. He hoped they'd been in time!

Mitch floated out over Jackie's trailer, hanging from the helicopter by a harness wrapped around his waist. Unfortunately he couldn't control where he was going. That was up to Matt, who was giving the pilot all the signals. If he could just get close enough to unhitch the trailer, maybe he could save Jackie. One false move...and she might be killed.

"Jackie!" he yelled as he got closer.

"Mitch!" she screamed from inside of the trailer. "Is that you?"

Good, Mitch thought. *She's still alive. So far.* He hovered over the metal hitch that attached the trailer to the car. If he could get close enough to pull the pin out, the car would plummet down to the rocks—and the trailer would stay on the cliff. It was worth a try. He had no other choices.

He swung back and forth above the hitch,

narrowly missing it several times in a row. He couldn't grab onto the hitch directly—if he did, his weight might be enough to pull the trailer down. He had to undo the hitch without putting his weight on it. Below him, the rocks seemed to get closer and closer. *Come on!* he thought, focusing all of his mental energy on the job. *Do it!*

Finally, his hands reached the hitch. He grasped the pin and pressed it down.

The car plunged down the side of the cliff, a rattling, clanging mess of metal and rubber. Finally, it crashed to a stop on the rocks at the ocean's edge.

The trailer seesawed back and forth, just barely hanging on to the edge of the cliff.

That's part one, Mitch thought, breathing a heavy sigh of relief. *So far, so good. Now for part two!*

Matt signaled the helicopter to swing Mitch around to the other side of the trailer, where the door was located. Unfortunately, the door was on the side of the trailer that was facing straight down.

"Jackie!" Mitch yelled. "Come to the door—slowly!"

Jackie opened the door, wearing a blue satin bathrobe. She gasped in terror as she looked out at the cliff.

"Don't look down!" Mitch told her quickly. He didn't even want to look down himself, and he was firmly supported in a harness—not standing in a trailer that was about to pitch onto the rocks below.

"Mitch!" Jackie shrieked, as the helicopter lowered him closer to her. She held out her hand, imploring him to help her, her body racked by sobs of terror.

"Hang on, we're going to get you out," Mitch said, reaching out for Jackie. He was having trouble grabbing hold of her because her hand was shaking so much. "Take it easy!" he said, reaching for her again.

Finally, the two of them clasped hands. Mitch slowly angled closer to the trailer. When he was right next to the door, he said, "Jackie, you're going to leap into my arms. Ready?"

She nodded.

"One, two…three!" Mitch said.

Jackie jumped, threw her arms around Mitch's shoulders, and clung to him. He held her legs with his hands and pushed off the trailer with his legs.

The helicopter lifted the two of them high into the air, swinging them away from the trailer. They hovered out over the water before being slowly brought around to a safe part of the cliff.

The helicopter set them down, and Mitch gently helped Jackie stand on her feet. Then he undid the harness and started to put it around Jackie so the helicopter could carry her back to the beach.

"Mitch, I—" Jackie threw her arms around Mitch once again and hugged him tightly.

"Don't say anything," he told her, stroking her long hair.

"Thank you," she whispered softly. "Thank you."

Stephanie was treading water behind Max and Tom, who were floating comfortably—if coldly—in their life vests. *Two in, four out*, she reminded herself, as she practiced her breathing, preparing to free-dive. *Two in...and four out.*

She remembered the feeling of Riley's arms around her the night before, as he taught her how to hold enough air in her lungs. She hadn't felt so close to someone in a long time. She really cared about Riley.

"What are you doing?" Max asked, looking over his shoulder at Stephanie as if she had lost her mind. "Meditating?"

"I'm going to go down after Riley," she told him calmly.

"He's over a hundred feet down there!" Max protested. "You won't have enough air to get back up! Besides, you can't leave us *alone* up here!"

"Shut up, Max," Tom groaned. "Let her try and save him, if she can!"

"Don't worry," Stephanie said. "Help is on the way. I'll be back soon." She placed her yel-low-rimmed mask over her face and adjusted it on her nose. Then, taking her last breaths in, she dove down to the ocean floor.

Using her swim fins to propel her, she quickly swam down, searching the entire area for any air bubbles that might be escaping from Riley. Finally she spotted his arm jutting out from underneath a pile of large rocks, clutching a flashlight. She peered in at Riley through the small gap in the rocks, and was relieved to find him still alive. She gave him the thumbs-up signal, trying to tell him he'd be all right.

He gazed back at her, his face masked with doubt.

CHAPTER THIRTEEN

Newman and Logan, wearing wetsuits, leapt off the Scarab into the water. Their rescue cans were strapped across their chests.

C.J. stared at the capsized motorboat. The geologists were floating beside it, wearing life vests. But where was Stephanie?

Logan and Newman swam quickly to the victims and guided them to the Scarab, where C.J. pulled them on board.

"Where's Stephanie?" she asked them.

"Down there," the older one told her, pointing to the water.

C.J. grabbed her swim fins and mask. She picked up two bottles of spare air—one for her and one for Stephanie. Then she plunged into the ocean.

Here I come, Stephanie! Hold on!

Riley held the regulator of his compressed air tank out to Stephanie. She grabbed it from him gratefully and took two deep breaths.

That would hold her a few more minutes.

Riley signaled for her to head back up to the surface. Stephanie didn't want to leave him there, but she knew that his air tank wouldn't hold him—never mind her—much longer.

She nodded, knowing it was the only thing to do. Pushing off from the rocks, she headed for the surface, her lungs burning. She didn't know if she could make it. She felt herself losing strength, as if she were swimming as hard as she could and getting absolutely nowhere.

Then, like a vision, just when her body was about to give out, she saw a flashlight heading toward her. Behind it was C.J.'s long blond hair, streaming out behind her in the ocean. She'd never been so relieved to see her friend before!

Of course C.J. came through for me, she thought. *She always does!*

C.J. pushed a bottle of spare air toward her. Stephanie put it into her mouth, gasping for her next breath.

Phew. That was a close one, she thought as she and C.J. headed up together. C.J. was half-towing her because Stephanie was so weak from lack of oxygen. *Now we have to come back for Riley.*

"Newman, get me a tank!" Stephanie said as soon as she was on the Scarab.

C.J. shook her head, her mask slipping a little from her head. "Stephanie, you're in no shape to go back down there."

"I'm fine!" Stephanie told her, even though she knew that wasn't completely true. "Riley doesn't have much air left." She rushed over to Newman. "Ready?"

Newman nodded.

"Let's go!" Stephanie said.

Logan started to pull on a tank, but C.J. put a hand on his arm.

"Forget your gear. Stay here with the geologists!" she said.

"No way!" Logan replied, shrugging her off. "I'm a lifeguard, not a baby-sitter." He cast a disapproving glance at Max and Tom, who were still recovering from their ordeal in the ocean.

"Well, if you're a lifeguard, then you know the deal. Lifeguards follow orders," C.J. said sternly. "Check your manual."

Logan frowned but kept quiet. He looked like a little kid who'd just been told he couldn't go on the roller coaster again.

C.J. didn't have time to sort out another guard's problems. If he couldn't do the job that was assigned to him, then maybe he didn't belong at Baywatch.

Just before C.J., Stephanie, Barnett, and New–

man were about to dive, Max managed to find the strength to stand up. He rushed over to them. "When you go down there, you have to retrieve the seismometer! It may have recorded vital information."

"If we can get it, we will, but it won't be our top priority," Stephanie told him, adjusting her tank.

Max grabbed her arm. "You *have* to make it a top priority! You don't understand!"

Stephanie gently removed his hand. "*You* don't understand. We're trying to save Riley's life. *That's* our top priority. And if you think about it, that should be everyone's top prior– ity." She gestured to Logan. "Logan, please take care of Max and Tom here."

Logan looked at Max and smiled. "I'll be glad to."

C.J. did a slow burn. "Come on, let's go," she said. "We don't have much time."

C.J., Stephanie, Barnett, and Newman all flipped backward off the boat into the water a few moments later. Stephanie swam down to the fault as quickly as she could. She knew C.J. was right: they didn't have a second more to waste.

Logan paced back and forth impatiently on the Scarab. There was nothing he hated more than not being in on a rescue. Why couldn't somebody else stay on the boat and play baby-sitter to these pathetic, whiny scientist guys?

Then he got an idea. If this Max person really wanted his precious seismometer... maybe the trip to save him wouldn't be a *total* waste after all.

"So," Logan said casually, strolling over to stand beside Max. The geologist was anxiously watching the spot where the four lifeguards had entered the water. "What's it worth to you?"

Max looked at him, confused. "What's *what* worth?"

"Your seismometer or whatever's down there," Logan said.

Max shook his head. "The information it has gathered is invaluable. If it's lost..." He shrugged helplessly.

"Invaluable, eh? Then you'd be willing to pay quite a bit to recover it, I guess." Logan waited, hoping Max would get the point.

The geologist nodded slowly, as if he understood.

"Hey, I'd be defying orders and maybe risking my life down there," Logan said. "I'm sure that's worth some sort of compensation...as well as your guarantee not to disclose our dealings?" He looked at Max expectantly.

A smile spread slowly across Max's face.

So, Logan thought. *Maybe these scientist guys aren't pathetic after all.*

Riley closed his eyes in despair. He didn't know how much longer he could wait. Stephanie had only been gone a few minutes, but now he was starting to wonder whether he'd even seen her at all. *Maybe I just imagined that*, he thought sadly. *Maybe I'm starting to see things.*

He knew that he was running out of air. The tank was nearly empty. He'd probably sucked every last molecule of oxygen out of it already. He took a breath in and held it as long as he could. He felt as if he was about to pass out.

Just then, almost miraculously, air bubbles appeared—and a second later, a face. Stephanie was back! She shoved a bottle of spare air at him.

From his position behind the rocks, Riley could just barely make out three other figures with her. They pushed and shoved at the rocks trapping him until they had made enough of a hole for Riley to get through.

He swam out, his arms and legs seriously cramped from being motionless so long. But he'd never felt more free in his entire life.

* * *

"You guys don't move, okay?" Logan told the geologists. "Don't go anywhere." He winked at Max and then dove off the Scarab. He was about to become the best–paid baby–sitter in all of Los Angeles.

Logan plunged into the ocean. All he had to do was grab the seismometer and get back before another aftershock hit. Max had described as closely as he could where Logan would find the instrument. He was confident he could get it before any aftershock could happen.

Two minutes of work…that's it. And I'll be very generously rewarded. Logan held a flashlight in one hand as he poked around corners and between rocks, brushing kelp and seaweed out of his way. In the other hand he held a tank of spare air, using it when he needed to.

He spotted the seismometer resting on some bedrock. It was easy enough to grab—it even had handles on the sides. *Isn't that convenient?* Logan thought, already swimming away from the dangerous fault area. *Those geologists think of everything, don't they?*

C.J. pulled herself up onto the Scarab, lifting her mask onto her head. Then she walked over to Max and Tom. "The lifeguard we left up here with you—he went after your seis-mometer, didn't he?"

Max shrugged. "I tried to stop him. But he said if the information it contained could save lives during future earthquakes...it was his obligation to get it."

C.J. frowned, shaking her head. "His obliga-tion was to do what he was told."

"Something Logan seems to have a lot of trouble with," Stephanie commented. She turned to Riley, who was standing beside her. "So how are you feeling?"

He gazed into her eyes. "I was afraid you hadn't made it back up last time."

Stephanie grinned. "What can I say? I had a great free-diving coach." She wrapped her arms around Riley's shoulders and hugged him tightly.

Just then, Logan surfaced, holding the seis-mometer in his left hand. He held it up tri-umphantly for everyone to see. "Got it!" he yelled.

"Great!" Max cried happily.

"Now *you're* going to get it," C.J. muttered under her breath to Stephanie.

"And how," Stephanie said, raising one eye-brow as Logan climbed over the edge of the boat.

Logan walked over to Max and handed him

the seismometer. "Hope you can recover what's in here. I know how *valuable* it is."

"Thank you," Max said, taking it from him. "I'm very grateful."

As soon as Logan had let go of the seismometer, Stephanie put her hand on his arm. "I need to have a word with my exchange lifeguard, if you don't mind," she told Max. Then, pulling Logan aside, she said, "Give me one reason I shouldn't exchange you straight back to Australia."

Logan shrugged. "You're right. I disregarded orders. I'm sorry."

Stephanie stared at him. Why didn't she buy this super-humble act he was putting on?

"But if even one life is saved by the information in that device, it was worth it," Logan continued.

Stephanie couldn't exactly argue with that, even though she knew Logan was only trying to snow her. "True," she said, "but you still should have stayed here to take care of these guys."

Logan nodded. "I'll accept whatever punishment you think I deserve."

Stephanie nodded thoughtfully. *Don't be so sure*, she told Logan silently. *Just wait until you hear what I have planned for you!*

CHAPTER FOURTEEN

Logan walked out of the men's room and onto the deck outside Baywatch headquarters, carrying a bucket of cleaning supplies. He sighed loudly.

"Now that's a job you're more suited for." Matt nodded as he walked up, grinning at Logan. "Do you do windows *and* sinks? Or just toilets?"

"What's your problem, mate?" Logan asked, turning around. He walked over to Matt and stood right in front of him, giving him a challenging look. "What have I ever done to you?"

Matt shrugged. "Lifeguards have to trust each other. And I don't trust you. That's the bottom line." He started to walk away, but then he stopped. There was something else on his mind. "And stay away from Caroline," he added.

"What's the matter? Are you afraid of a little healthy competition?" Logan scoffed.

Competition? Matt thought. *Hardly.* "Look, Caroline's real vulnerable right now. She's been hurt. I don't want her hurt again, especially not by someone like you."

Logan set the container of supplies on the deck railing. "Just for the record, I am not *interested* in Caroline. And if I was, it would be none of your business. No, I intend to find a rich, beautiful Malibu woman who'll take care of my every need." He grinned. "After all, this *is* the land of opportunity, isn't it?"

Matt couldn't believe the utter arrogance of this guy. As if a rich, beautiful woman would even *want* a second-rate loser lifeguard like Logan. "Yeah, well—don't miss the opportunity to clean the rest of the bathrooms around here." He smiled at Logan and walked away.

Downstairs, at the first aid center of Baywatch headquarters, Caroline handed an ice pack to an injured man. "Okay, now. I want you to keep this on your knee until the swelling goes down."

"Thanks," he told her.

"You're welcome," Caroline told him. She was really enjoying helping at the first aid center. She and Hobie had brought Garrick in right after she revived him. Just thinking of the satisfied feeling she'd gotten when Garrick started breathing on his own again made Car–

oline smile to herself. When she was helping people like that, she felt so...complete, as if what she was doing really mattered.

"Caroline! Are you all right?"

Caroline whirled around, surprised to see Stephanie standing behind her. She'd heard over the radio that her sister was okay, but seeing her in person was even better. She hugged Stephanie tightly. "Me? Oh, Stephanie, I was scared to death about *you*," Caroline replied. "I'm so glad you're all right!"

"I'm fine," Stephanie said. She stepped back slightly. "You remember Riley?"

"Sure." Caroline nodded. "I'm so glad every-thing turned out okay."

Riley smiled at Stephanie. "Thanks to your sister."

"Everybody did their part," Stephanie said, her face turning a little pink.

Caroline couldn't believe it. Her sister never blushed—for anyone. She must really like this guy. Caroline knew how close people could become when they worked together...espe-cially when they were working to save lives.

Just then, Caroline spotted Mitch coming down the stairs. "Excuse me for a second," she said to Stephanie and Riley. Not that it mat-tered if she left—they only seemed aware of each other right now.

"Mitch!" Caroline called, rushing up to him. "Listen, I just wanted to let you know how proud you would have been of Hobie today. He went under the pier to save a man's life. I know he was scared, Mitch, but he did it any–way."

Mitch glanced around the crowded room. "I've been looking all over for Hobie. Where is he?"

Caroline gestured in the direction of the beach.

Mitch nodded. "Thanks. I'll go catch up with him."

Hobie crouched in the sand, examining the newest wing he'd added to a giant sand castle. He hadn't built a castle like this for a long, long time.

We might as well all be living in castles made of sand, he thought, pressing another bucketful of wet sand around the foundation. *Our whole lives can fall apart and wash away at any second.* Hobie stood up and started scooping out one of the towers.

"Hey, that's the best castle you've ever done." Mitch came up behind him and crouched down beside the sand castle.

"Thanks." Hobie stood back, admiring his work. All it needed now was a moat.

"You know, Caroline told me about that guy under the pier." Mitch watched Hobie carefully. "That took a lot of courage."

Hobie focused on the top level of the castle, smoothing over one of the turrets with his sculpting tool—a discarded ice cream stick. "I was pretty scared the whole time."

"I'm sure you were," Mitch said casually. "Who wouldn't have been?"

Hobie wheeled around, staring at his father. How could he not understand? "No, I mean I was *real* scared. I was a total wimp!" he cried. "I never want to go near that place again!"

His father recoiled, looking hurt. "Hobe, it's okay to be scared sometimes. Look, I know that's how you feel right now," he said. "But in a few days—"

"I won't even *be* here in a few days. I'm outta here—I'm history!" Hobie declared. "And you have to come, too. Dad, we can't live here in California anymore! We've got to move away!"

Mitch stared at him in disbelief. "Just pack up and leave? Just like that?"

Hobie nodded vigorously. "Yes."

"Leave everything behind...and start a new life someplace else?" Mitch asked.

"At least we'll *have* lives!" Hobie said. "We won't have to worry about being crushed by buildings falling all around us."

Mitch didn't answer. *How could he?* Hobie thought. *He can't possibly disagree with me. I know I'm right—I'm totally right!*

"Dad," Hobie said finally. "I'm still a wimp. I can't stop shaking all the time."

"That's normal, pal," Mitch said. He went over and put an arm around Hobie's shoulders.

"Hobe...there are things to be scared of every minute of every day. Anywhere you live. But if you're prepared—"

"How can you be prepared for an earthquake that can happen at any time?" Hobie pointed out. "They said on the news that there'd probably be five *thousand* aftershocks. And that this quake wasn't even the *big* one!"

"I understand how you feel, buddy," Mitch said. "A lot of people here are feeling the same things today, all over Los Angeles—all over California."

Hobie turned to the sand castle and smashed his fists into it, crushing the whole thing with his hands.

Mitch grabbed his shoulders and shook him. "Hobie! Hobie, it's okay!" he said urgently. "Everything's going to be fine. You were a hero today!"

"Do you really think so?" Hobie asked, so

114

softly that he could barely hear himself.

"I really do," Mitch said.

Hobie stared out at the ocean. "Dad? Is it okay if I go on a short trip or something? Like, to visit Mom?" he asked.

"Sure," Mitch said. "But you can't be gone too long. You need to get back in time to be a junior guard this summer." He grinned at Hobie.

"But I'm not—" Hobie began to protest. He had planned on playing with his band all summer. But he had saved someone's life today. Maybe he *was* kind of a hero. Maybe he'd even be as good a lifeguard as his dad someday. He could still play with the band, even if he wouldn't have a lot of free time. And a whole summer hanging out on the beach with all those gorgeous girls just dying to meet him... "Actually, junior guards sounds kind of good right now."

"See? Maybe that earthquake wasn't *all* bad," Mitch teased.

Hobie grabbed a handful of sand and stuffed it down his dad's shirt.

Soon, they were chasing each other down the beach, tossing sand and kicking water at each other, as if nothing had ever happened.

But Hobie wouldn't forget the earthquake, or all the people who'd been hurt. And next time he'd be ready if another "big one" hit the city. Maybe next time he'd be a real life-guard...and he could make a real difference, saving lives. Just like his dad.

On the other hand, there *was* another option. When the next big earthquake hit L.A., maybe he'd be living in New York City, or Paris, as a major rock star...

Hey, it could happen, he told himself, grinning as he jogged beside his dad. But right now, he'd be happy hanging out at Baywatch.

BAYWATCH™
LIFEGUARD LINGO

rescue board – a large, wide surfboard over ten feet long, usually with handles, used to make rescues; also known as a paddle board.

rescue breathing – resuscitation of a non-breathing victim by blowing air from the mouth of the rescuer into a non-breathing victim's airway; also known as mouth-to-mouth.

rescue buoy – cylindrical floatation device with handles, which can be towed by a lifeguard using an attached line and harness, used to effect a swimming rescue; modern rescue buoys are made of hard plastic; also known as a torpedo buoy, torp, can, or can buoy.

rescue tube – a flexible, foam rubber rescue flotation device which can be wrapped around a victim's chest, fastened, and used by a lifeguard to tow the victim to safety.

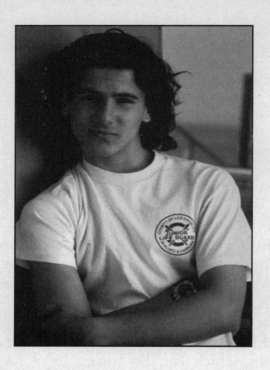

Hobie Buchannon is the son of Mitch Buchannon, Los Angeles lifeguard lieutenant, at Baywatch. A native of L.A., Hobie's dream is to follow in his dad's footsteps as a lifeguard, or maybe to be a rock star! He enjoys skating on the pier with his friends, jamming with his band, and helping save lives at Baywatch!

JUNIOR LIFEGUARD #1
BAYWATCH™

HOBIE GETS A LIFE

Lifeguard training…or the real thing?

"Hit the water, hit the water, swim around the buoy and back!" Summer shouted to the group of Junior Lifeguards running toward her. She started the stopwatch in her hand.

Hobie high-stepped into the surf, and dived under the first big wave. Lauren was right behind him. He hesitated a second, waiting for her to catch up before swimming toward the buoy placed fifty yards from shore.

Suddenly Lauren stopped swimming—right in front of him.

"Are you all right?" Hobie asked, staring at Lauren. Her arms weren't moving, and her legs had completely stopped kicking. She wasn't even treading water!

"Lauren!" Hobie cried.

But Lauren didn't seem to hear, as she slipped beneath the surface…

BAYWATCH™ #1

INFATUATIONS

Mitch Buchannon to the rescue...

Mitch quickly spotted the submerged victim. Her white dress had an eerie glow in the dark water.

Immediately, Mitch dived straight for her.

As he got closer, he saw that she was young–no more than twenty.

Wrapping a strong arm around her waist, he brought her to the surface. Stephanie was paddling the long board toward him. With her help, he laid the unconscious young woman onto the board and began to paddle back to shore. Stephanie followed, swimming close behind.

Mitch carried the victim out of the water and laid her on the hard–packed sand. He knelt beside her and put his ear to her mouth, listening for sounds of breathing.

Stephanie took the young woman's wrist in her hand and placed two fingers across it.

"I've got a strong pulse," she told Mitch.

"C'mon," Mitch murmured urgently. He took a breath of air and sealed his mouth over the victim's. *She's too young to die,* Mitch thought. *Way too young...*

BAYWATCH™ #2
WET 'N' WILD

Trouble was Neely's middle name...

Before Matt knew what had hit him, Neely's mouth closed over his. It took a moment for him to react, but he finally broke from the kiss and slid away from Neely.

"Neely, no," he said firmly. "This isn't a good idea, okay?"

"You're right. We're on duty," she said, stepping close to Matt again and placing a hand on his bare shoulder. "But tonight after work, we can go out and pick up where we left off."

"Neely, first of all, one of us should be watching the water at all times," Matt said. "Secondly, I can't see you tonight, or any other night, because C.J. and I are–"

"C.J.? C. J. Parker? That girl who introduced us?"

"Yes," said Matt. "Sorry, Neely...but I really care about C.J., you know?"

"Oh, I see," said Neely, looking at the ground. But she wasn't going to give up on Matt that easily...

BAYWATCH™

Join the Baywatch Fan Club!

For more information, write to:

Baywatch Beach Club
P.O. Box 69249
Los Angeles, CA 90069